THE UNSPEAKABLES

Peter F. Jemison

Best Wishes, Magpie

Peter Jemison

On 10·4·17

Published by New Generation Publishing in 2015

Copyright © Peter F. Jemison 2015

First Edition

The author asserts the moral right under the Copyright, Designs and Patents Act 1988 to be identified as the author of this work.

All Rights reserved. No part of this publication may be reproduced, stored in a retrieval system or transmitted, in any form or by any means without the prior consent of the author, nor be otherwise circulated in any form of binding or cover other than that which it is published and without a similar condition being imposed on the subsequent purchaser.

www.newgeneration-publishing.com

 New Generation Publishing

*

"The English country gentleman galloping after a fox
- the unspeakable in full pursuit of the uneatable"

Oscar Wilde: A Woman of No Importance

*

Also by Peter F Jemison:

The Causio Contracts

Castle Douglas

PREFACE

It's 2012 and foxes are still being hunted despite the Ban. A stalwart in animal protection, Iain Lauder is systematically staging a novel form of protest against the main perpetrators. His identity is discovered, pitching Lauder and his fiancée into a maelstrom of violence, drugs and murder.

CHAPTER ONE

The farmhouse occupied the crown of the hill. It was a stark, two-storey building in weathered sandstone with a large barn on one side. On the other a copse of firs, angling down the flank of the hill, protected the house from the north.

Lauder sat on a hummock in the small wood, surveying the scene. Positioned as he was at the bottom extremity of the trees, he could just discern the outline of the house above him and yet was effectively screened from the side road a few yards away. He'd taken good care not to use the road on his three mile trek from the village; sometimes stumbling into ditches, tripping over fallen branches, once fording a small stream, he'd used every bit of cover in the shape of hedgerows and trees during the approach to his present position. There had been one walker on the lane, exercising a rowdy little Scottie, and apparently returning to the village. But from behind a stand of closely packed pine he'd watched both go past unobserved.

It was a lovely evening in this part of mid-Northumberland. The wind had dropped, and so far the gathering twilight had not obscured the undulating ground, the long views of wood and fell rising toward a pale blue sky. Lauder glanced sideways at the myriad of sheep scattered across the fields sloping up to the farmhouse. A rural idyll indeed, but one he mustn't upset when he made his first move. The last thing he wanted was a herd of sheep bleating and panicking as he worked toward the top of the hill. The best course, he resolved, would be to make his way hugging the perimeter fence; once it became dark the risk of making a noise in the wood would be too great.

Ten minutes later the light was all but gone. The sky had assumed a deep purple colour only relieved by a flickering rim of orange on its western edge. In the thickening gloom the sheep had become grey indistinct shapes, and a couple of lamps were showing from the downstairs windows of the farmhouse. Lauder delved into the canvas bag beside him. He withdrew a dark green balaclava and pulled it over his balding head. Next he removed two half-bricks from the bag and then stuffed it firmly into the pocket of his Barbour jacket. That done, he gripped a brick in each hand, looked both ways along the road to see no-one was coming, then ducked between two wooden slats of the fence.

He moved cautiously along the edge of the wood. With the trees behind him he knew he couldn't be seen. It would be later when he had to move into the open that the fun and games might start. For the conditions weren't ideal – a bright half-moon had appeared, and glancing sideways down the sloping hill, his line of retreat, he realised he would sometimes be silhouetted.

Nevertheless, Mr and Mrs Dodds, prosperous farmers and part of the local Hunt's nucleus, were about to get his calling cards. The two half-bricks he brandished had foolscap notices elasticated to them. Each bore the acronym SPFC, and then graphically insulting comments on the lineage and behaviour of the imminent recipients. Lauder was occasionally appalled at what he wrote. But then the memory of a horrendous scene near his home would revive: a beautiful vixen first at bay against the stone wall of a field, and then the arterial blood fountaining into the air as she was engulfed by a pack of snarling, baying hounds.

Presumably the inestimable Mr and Mrs Dodds were there that day. If not, there had undoubtedly been many others in which they featured. In which case the terrible crashes of two half-bricks thrown onto their roof, followed by the scream and judder of protesting slates as the objects slid earthwards, would be only partially what they deserved.

Unless the dog spoilt his script. He had seen the animal yesterday while sizing up the place. An overfed spaniel cavorting at the feet of a lumpy figure he took to be Mrs Dodds, returning from a walk. Neither of them had seen him – he was half a mile away, watching through binoculars. But now he couldn't be sure where the dog was, and he no longer had the luxury of distance.

Glancing nervously around him, Lauder left the comfort of the trees and moved along the brow of the hill in a line parallel to the house. He came to a stop in front of a central wooden gate leading onto a small garden. The room to the left of the front door was in darkness. But light shone through the curtained windows of the one on the right, and he thought he could hear the murmur of a television set. Otherwise there was silence: no growling dog emerging from the corners of the building, no beginnings of an angry protest from within..

He bent slowly down and placed the half brick in his left hand on the ground. He straightened, then, arching his back, threw right-handed upwards with all his strength. Immediately he repeated the process – swooping down to grasp the other brick even before the first crash came. When it did, rupturing the night air with its intensity, the second brick was already on an upward parabola.

Lauder turned and began to run. He'd almost reached full pace when the second crashing impact occurred. He snatched a look over his shoulder to see one of the upstairs lights flick on, just as a dog began barking. Sheep were scattering in front of him, running and barging into one another, their raucous racket filling his ears. His breath was coming faster now, his heart hammering, and he wrenched the balaclava from his head in mid-stride.

He was perhaps a hundred and fifty yards from the house, angling down toward the road, when the shot came, the distinctive crack of what could only be a shot gun. Fear drove Lauder even faster. The lie of the land helping him, the sweat cascading from his brow, he launched into a lung-bursting sprint. He had to get out of the fields, the open – the feeling between his shoulder blades demanded no less. He started to weave, racing for the grey blur of the gate below him.

Gasping with exertion, Lauder arrived at the gate and

hauled himself onto the first rung. He snatched another look back. The shape of a Land Rover was silhouetted against the night sky. The hollows and mounds of the terrain were causing its headlights to oscillate wildly as the vehicle began to trundle down the slope.

Lauder threw himself over the gate. He staggered to his feet, the jarring a further toll on his already depleted state, and limped across the road. Then he was through a gap in the hedge he'd spotted an hour earlier, and one last stumbling run across a narrow tract of land brought him to the wonderful refuge of some trees.

His breathing gradually returning to normal, Lauder sat behind a bush about ten yards into the blackness of the wood. He could see the headlights of the Land Rover in the field across the lane manoeuvring one way and then another, still searching for him. Clearly his athletics in vaulting the gate had gone unnoticed.

Well, they were facing a hopeless task in locating him now. His lean face relaxed as he recalled the words of his NCO from long ago, "Give me some blacking, a dark wood, and I could sit a few yards away from you 'Charlies' all night and you'd never know it." Lauder glanced down, barely able to register the hands in front of him. The remark was proving prophetic – for the time being at least, it seemed he was out of harm's way.

Nevertheless, it had been a damned close call, he mused. Though he knew he might meet that sort of retaliation one night, the actuality had thoroughly shaken him. He hadn't bargained on such a quick reaction – the Dodds had been expecting trouble. The law required a shot gun to be dismantled and kept locked away, not propped up in the corner of a living room ready for action.

Yet on the reverse side, he told himself, a grim smile appearing, it was symptomatic of how much he was rattling them. The violent response, whether a warning shot or a deliberate attempt to disable him, was indicative of the neurosis he was creating. He was spoiling their life styles, letting them know that even in the heart of their homes they could no longer think themselves safe. The nocturnal raids – this was his fifth in the last three months – must now be the subject of heated and alarmed discussions in the local Conservative club or wherever the bastards gathered.

A section of the wood to the right of him, about fifteen yards away, was suddenly illuminated. Lauder tensed, thinking his line of escape had been spotted after all. But then he saw the Land Rover was emerging from the fields. It turned onto the road in the direction of the village, and the driver got out, leaving the engine idling. He walked a little way ahead of the vehicle and was joined by a second man, who'd been closing the gate.

Lauder couldn't see the figures of men now; they were behind a particularly dense stretch of the roadside hedge. But they were almost opposite him, and with the light breeze drifting his way he could overhear them quite plainly above the flat hum of the vehicle's diesel engine.

"The bastard could be anywhere, Bill." a voice said; the words clipped and brittle, the anger unmistakable.

"There might be more than one, Mr Dodds," the second man said in a broad Northumbrian accent, the tone deferential.

"I want the bugger who bricked our roof, Bill – he's put Mollie in a hell of a state. It's only a pity I didn't get to the door ten seconds earlier; the shot was just too long for the Purdey"

"We could try the village Mr Dodds. See if anybody's noticed strangers there

"I suppose so – we can't run round like wet hens all night. C'mon, we'll call on Clive Henshaw too. I've had enough of this. Something's got to be done, and bloody quickly!"

Lauder heard two doors slam and the Land Rover moved off. He rose somewhat stiffly to his feet. The motionless wait in the cold night air with perspiration drying on his body had left him quite chilled. He stamped his feet and waved his arms, feeling the circulation gradually improving.

Nothing he'd overheard gave him undue cause for concern. His Vauxhall was in the car park of the pub on the outskirts of the village. There'd been a few other cars there when he left it early evening, and now, he glanced at the luminous hands of his wrist watch, at twenty-five to nine almost two hours later, there should be even more. A middle-aged man seemingly hurrying from the environs of the pub to his car wouldn't cause comment. Besides they were probably looking for a much younger man, someone more typical of those who openly harassed the Hunt over the autumn and winter months.

The only remaining risk, as he saw it, would be if he were spotted on the way back to the village. To be framed in the headlights of a passing motorist, or to meet another nocturnal walker, were possibilities he must avoid. He couldn't take the slightest chance of his identity being compromised. So there was no option but the overland route again. It would mean striking out to the far side of the wood where he was, followed by some fairly rough walking over several cultivated fields. But that way the most risk he ran was turning an ankle or wetting his feet in the small brook he knew he must cross.

*

Lauder particularly liked his study: at night it was his favourite place in the house. There was another dark brown leather armchair besides the one he occupied, a pine book-case stacked to almost ceiling height and his computer desk. Two lamps in opposite corners gave the room a warm, compact feel, bringing out the rich browns of the soft furnishings, highlighting the original watercolour, a landscape, above the stone fireplace.

He stretched his legs out to the warmth of the gas fire. He had exchanged his rather grubby outdoor clothes for a fair-isle sweater, beige pants and a pair of old but comfortable shoes when he returned twenty minutes ago. It was nearly ten-thirty, and his two black cats, Sally and Sophie, were still vying with one another to show their pleasure at his presence. Sally, the older and more dominant of the two, had settled herself on his lap purring continuously, while Sophie, perched on the armchair just behind his head, was nuzzling his neck at ten second intervals. He sipped his single malt reflectively, his attention occasionally diverted by some item being relayed on the late evening television news.

The journey back had been uneventful. He had worked through a copse and crossed four fields of what appeared in the pale moonlight to be barley, growing no more than ankle high. Then, guided by the ever-brightening lights of the public house, he'd negotiated a pasture where a small herd of cows was haunched down for the night; and finally, after climbing a five-bar gate, had arrived at the Vauxhall. No-one had noticed him; there'd been no-one around to notice him. So a mere ten minutes later he was home and garaging the car.

Lauder smiled to himself; all in all it had been a successful night. The incident of the gun shot had sent his adrenalin levels soaring, of course. But he'd racked up the pressure on the die-hards in the Hunt once again, achieved just what he set out to do. Dodds' obvious agitation, the allusion to Mollie being on the brink of wetting her pants, the urgency in consulting the master, Henshaw, for whatever inspiration he might bring to the problem: all pointed to one conclusion. Namely, he was beginning to win.

It has been his second night raid in as many weeks. The last was when he'd walked into the grounds of the area's MP - a man who knew foxes were being killed but kept 'schtum' – and fixed abusive notices to some of the windows, the gate posts and the front door. There had been no immediate retaliation, no clamour of enraged voices that night. His victims had slept undisturbed. But he was sure they wouldn't have remained undisturbed the following morning; the waves of alarm, reinforcing those he'd already caused, spreading to every person still participating in the Hunt.

And now, once the latest news travelled, they would have even more to worry about. He was compounding the anxiety, building the myth of someone who could molest them at will. A someone who came in the night, bludgeoned their privacy, security and self-esteem, and then just as abruptly left. Little wonder Dodds now kept a shotgun next to his armchair. The awful question occupying their minds must be how long before the fiend started bludgeoning them!

A wave of tiredness suddenly swept over Lauder. He rose to his feet, stifling a yawn. The nervous tension of the night had finally leaked out, leaving him bone weary. He drained the last of his whisky while the cats meowed and circled around him. It was 'Whiskas' time – the nightly treat before they were relegated to their baskets in the porch....

CHAPTER TWO

"I wish Ralph had some sort of bloody system." Clive Henshaw groused, his feet searching for space on the crowded desk as he sprawled, legs extended, in a large, leather-bound armchair.

"What a dump this place is," he added as he looked at the sagging book shelves and the half open cabinet bulging with files. "No wonder our party affairs are in a mess. No wonder we don't know who all our members are!"

He disentangled his feet from the piles of paper and stacks of files spread over the desk's surface, and rose to his feet. He walked across the poky office of the local Conservative Association, the corners of his mouth still turned down in a scowl, and stood in front of a two-bar electric fire.

Dodds eyed the town's main butcher, and present Master of the Hunt, silently from his chair in front of the desk. Theirs was an uneasy but necessary alliance. As second in command with still a few years to wait he had to work with the man. But as he sat watching Henshaw, plainly on the brink of carping again, he was hard put to stop his dislike surfacing. The thickset figure, the close-cropped greying hair, the square face with the beginnings of a double chin, the protruding eyes – all combining to given an air of barely concealed belligerence, invariably had that effect on him.

"That's for the back burner for the moment," he eventually said. "More importantly, what are we going to do about last night?"

"Nothing," Henshaw said emphatically.

"Nothing!" Dodds echoed sharply. "Mollie's at her wits end and you say we do nothing. What do you mean?"

"Oh, for Christ's sake, Nigel," Henshaw said roughly, "what can we do? We senior people can't run around like headless chickens. We've got to keep our nerve, set an example and wait."

"Wait!" Dodds exclaimed, the slab of his face reddening. "Wait for what? Our numbers since that bastard Blair got his way have free-fallen from eighty to about twenty-five. If we don't do something there won't be any of us left before long; already two or three more are talking about not riding with us again."

"I know," Henshaw snorted, "you don't need to tell me. The lily-livered buggers make me sick. But there's no way I'm going to be stampeded."

Dodds stared at the stocky figure, dressed in checked pants and crimson sweater, blocking out the electric fire in front of him. The man's insensitive, unsympathetic attitude was really annoying him.

"Alright," he said, trying to keep his temper under control. "Tell me what you've got in mind."

"I'm sure it's one man," Henshaw replied. "I've talked to all the people who've been raided, and what comes out is a pattern of careful preparation and planning."

"But...," Dodds began to interject.

Henshaw imperiously waved him into silence. "That to me means the swine's got no back up – he's operating alone, and incidentally because of that is doubly effective. Do you remember the bagged fox job about two months ago?"

"At the Smith's farm near Redesmouth. I wasn't there but I heard about it."

"Well, he dropped Tod right outside the front door; a road kill, a dog fox of about fourteen pounds. He must have lugged the bag across the patio while we were all gin and tonicing it inside. It took nerve," Henshaw said grudgingly, shaking his head, "someone only needed to look out of a window."

"And?" Dodds said sharply.

"I'm getting to it if you'll bloody let me....! We found all his calling cards, those fucking notices, scattered on the lane. He must have known he was riding his luck. Running out of time. So when he went back to his car after dropping Tod he must have tried to throw them over the front gate. But the wind caught them."

"So....?" Dodds said, his tone still cutting.

Henshaw studied the man for a moment, his expression sour. The face he saw wasn't prepossessing. It was white, verging on light grey, the colour somehow accentuated by the brown hair, the dark double-breasted blazer. The shape was flat – a broad forehead with cheeks and chin in the same plane, the only relief the nose splayed and wide in keeping with the rest of the face. The overall effect was one of deadness, but the beady eyes glaring at him were alive, and hot with impatience.

"You don't think, do you, Nigel," he said sneeringly. "You're so busy taking yourself seriously – swanning around as the country gentleman, the upmarket farmer that you rarely, if ever, think. This bastard is independent, not your usual saboteur or animal rights looney, and I can't get you to see it. By Christ you're such a waste of space – everything needs spelling out to you!"

Dodds bulky frame visibly shook. "Now look here, Henshaw...." he began to bluster, when the door opened.

James Davidson, the Conservative MP for the constituency, entered the room. He was good at entering, was Davidson; tall with blue eyes and silvery hair, always impeccably dressed – this time in a superbly-cut dark blue suit – he invariably made an impact and knew it.

If he detected a strain in the air he ignored it, and placing a black leather brief-case on the nearest chair, he extended a hand to both Henshaw and Dodds. "Damned shuttle was half an hour late into Newcastle," he murmured. "I hope I haven't kept you gentlemen waiting too long."

"There's nothing spoiling, James." Henshaw drily observed.

"Fine," Davidson said, glancing affably from one to another. "I've asked the steward to bring some drinks up – we've got to keep the working class working, you know." He smiled broadly.

There was a knock on the door, and in came a small

bald man. He was carrying a tray on which there was a bottle of whisky, three glasses and a pitcher of ice cubes.

"Excellent, Terry," Davidson beamed. "The advantages of sharing a premises with the Club never cease to amaze me. Put it on the desk over there if you can find room." He then signed the chit which the steward produced, and with a slight nod at Henshaw and Dodds the man left the office.

"This is very generous of you, James," Dodds said awkwardly, still inwardly boiling at Henshaw's words.

"Aah, my dear chap," Davidson said heartedly. "What are expenses for?" He moved to the desk and began pouring large measures of the whisky, handing the glasses out to each in turn.

"You'll have heard what happened last night," Henshaw said, despatching half a mouthful of his drink.

"Yes," Davidson nodded. "Ralph mentioned it on the phone this morning. It's bad business and none of us seem to be safe from this type of predation."

He glanced sympathetically at Dodds as he began to sip his whisky. "Mollie must be upset. I know Joan was when the bugger left his calling cards, and a brick on the bonnet of my Land Rover. The inference was plain – the next one through the windscreen."

"There must be something we can do," Dodds burst out, raising his free arm imploringly. "What about Alan Brett?... he used to ride with us. He's an ex-chief constable isn't he – surely he can help!"

Henshaw looked scathingly at Dodds. "Tell him, James, will you," he said tersely.

"It would be extremely damaging, Nigel," Davidson said levelly; "we're not the subject of anything like the attention we once received, and we want to keep it like that. If word got out about the nocturnal marauder Joe Public might be sufficiently diverted from the X Factor and its brainless 'celebrities' to raise questions as to why this individual was so upset with us. Then it doesn't take much imagination to see the 'antis' pitching in, and steering public thinking into the belief that the bloodthirsty

Hunt had reverted to its old ways despite it being against the law of the land."

The MP paused to look at the expressionless faces of Dodds and Henshaw. "It's absolute rubbish of course, I hugely sympathise with people like yourselves, who have to deal weekly during the season with the terrible constraints put upon you by the Act. It's an awful piece of legislation – monstrously unfair, badly drafted and basically unworkable. Having ridden with the Hunt in my younger days, I can quite see the hounds rampaging across this big wonderful county we have the privilege of living in, coming upon a real trail. Then how difficult it must be to reassert control over them, particularly when a fox is streaking away in the distance. But control we must, because the Act – which we will abolish sooner rather than later – doesn't make any allowances at all for the circumstances under which an animal is killed."

"Where does that leave us?" Dodds said harshly.

"Christ give me strength!" Henshaw exclaimed, raising his eyes to the ceiling.

"Don't you understand what James is saying, we haven't got to start trouble, we must bloody well prevent it!"

Davidson glanced at Henshaw, a brief flicker of distaste appearing on the unlined face. "Come now, Nigel don't you see," he said almost soothingly. "At the risk of repeating myself, it's paramount we keep the public spotlight off ourselves. If we inform the police now think of the reaction to much stretched resources being diverted to guard the homes of leading huntsmen. I'm, sure it would be taken up by regional TV and that would be self-escalating. No...., we're not news anymore and that's the way we want to keep it. We deal with the matter ourselves, and when the bugger is caught we involve the police. There is a world of difference between charging someone with trespass and malicious damage at a single farm, and bringing the same charges in respect of several farms. One speaks of an unknown settling a grudge, the other of a series of planned protests with all the undesirable conjecture that would arouse..."

Davidson stopped to look enquiringly at the two huntsmen, but neither spoke. "And now," he said, glancing down at his watch, " I must dash, as I indicated earlier today. Because of a dinner engagement this could only be a fleeting visit."

"We appreciate you coming in, James," Henshaw said. He looked balefully at Dodds for a moment. "What you've said makes sense."

"It's a wretched business, and I hope I've been helpful," The MP replied, then stepping forward he shook both their hands, picked up his briefcase and turned to leave.

"Typical confounded politician," Dodds remarked seconds after the office door had shut, "Can talk the birds down from the trees, but miles short on the action line."

"What the hell's the matter with you?" Henshaw demanded. "Davidson is a good MP. The Ban would have arrived about three years earlier in Labour's term but for him. Don't you remember that late night stunt he pulled of reading from a London telephone directory until the time for the Private Member's Bill ran out?"

Dodds glared at him as he walked to the bottle and half filled his tumbler. "It's damned well alright for you, isn't it? Your wife and home haven't been the target of a raid so far. You'd change your tune if it had happened to you – start reacting."

"We are reacting. We wait for the twat to make a mistake. He can't go on forever and not make a rick. Then one of us will get a good view of him, or a car registration number."

"And then?" Dodds insisted.

"Just leave it to me," Henshaw said darkly. "Kerr, Golightly and I will settle the bugger's hash....make him pay twice over for what he's done."

For the first time that night Dodds' face relaxed. He let the whisky rinse around his mouth, savouring the taste.

"You'd better not let James hear you talking like that," he said.

Henshaw grinned evilly. "I won't Nigel, I won't......" he almost whispered.

*

Meanwhile the subject of their conversation was driving on the A68 to his home in the little village of Culwell, ten miles north of Hexham. Davidson was glad to be free of that bully, Henshaw, and his dim-witted lieutenant, Dodds. He'd lied about a dinner engagement. After a busy week in the House and faced with various constituency duties over the weekend the idea of spending much of Friday night in the company of those two was an anathema. Besides what could he do about this blasted activist? The man was certainly protesting against what they were doing, or more precisely what they shouldn't be doing. If he'd owned any lingering doubts about them disobeying the law, taking advantage of the hounds coming across a real trail, they were now dispelled. Their demeanour at junctures in the meeting spoke volumes. It seemed Henshaw and his followers were impervious to the fact there'd been two prosecutions of 'rogue' Hunts – as the media were fond of calling them – already in the south. Anyway the remedy was plain and one he had been at pains to impress upon them. In short: stop the covert activities, be patient until hunting rights were restored and the problem would disappear!

The only son of a Cumbrian vicar – who in turn had been the second son of a prosperous grain merchant just after the First World War – he felt as if he'd been involved with, and surrounded by, farmers and landowners all his conscious life. There'd been four years in the mid-seventies, when studying Economics at Manchester University it seemed new perspectives were opening to him. But meeting his future wife, Joan, in the first year, the rigours of the course plus his then awkward reticence, had combined, causing much of the rich experience, the forging of any lasting relationships, to bypass him. Not for him the bawdy camaraderie of the student's union, the impassioned debates about the issues of the day, the indulgence of the new sexual liberty: although seldom directly, he was called Gentleman Jim by his peers, a young man apart, with Joan never far from his side.

And then it was fifteen dull, dry years – more landowners, more farmers and their ilk in a Penrith accountancy practice. The well-structured life firmly established, Joan now mother to two delightful little girls, and he becoming a heavyweight contender in the Conservative arena of local government. The map ahead yawningly clear – a senior partnership in the offing, his Sunday morning golf partners a GP and a land agent seemingly till they all dropped. He could even envisage the epitaph on his gravestone and what would be said about him in the funeral service.

Then, suddenly, excitingly, a call from London, central office, heralding a wider road and one which wasn't straight and featureless....Deliverance.... 'There was an unexpected vacancy', the voice said....The sitting MP had blemished his copy book, been deselected for extraordinarily bad form and bringing the party into disrepute. They were aware of the sterling work he'd done and therefore would he allow his name to go forward....

A couple of days later he learned from the same source that the thoroughly bad fellow had been importuning outside public toilets, and what made it worse they hadn't even been ladies' toilets... The good news was the constituency was the third safest for the Conservatives throughout the country, the indifferent news the seat was in the rolling land of West Northumberland, and therefore like some of Cumbria a bastion for the 'Hang-em-High, Tallyho and Kick-em-Out' brigade, namely more landowners, farmers and their like. Nevertheless, his pleasure, anticipation of the new breadth his life was promising, was only a little tinged, and once he'd prevailed in what was a formality of a selection process he grasped the opportunity wholeheartedly.

Now almost twenty years on, the progress, the breadth he'd hoped for had proved illusory. He'd made a bright start on the back-benches of Major's government, speaking authoritatively on the rural economy, and once, in particular, winning the approval of the hierarchy by complaining about the millions the banks were making at the expense of British livestock exporters due to the UK being outside the euro.

His europhile inclinations might have stood him in good stead had Major been elected to another term. But the public had found the party out, with his own majority diving to a mere fifteen hundred. The ghastly spectacle of 'cash for questions', the open and ongoing strife over the EEC, the intolerance of anything other than heterosexual behaviour – sometimes the subject of cheap jokes in the Common rooms – landed the charismatic Blair an easy passage into power.

Then thirteen years in opposition. The good impression he'd first made dwindling as the young, sharp-suited millionaires gradually replaced the old guard on the shadow front benches; and he himself undergoing a change, a new mind-set during that period. Perhaps triggered by one of the more jingoistic ministers disparagingly referring to him as 'the darling of the euro', he became less active in the House; concentrating increasingly on himself – he attended fewer sittings, acquired two executive directorships and creatively massaging the lax expenses system gained a nice 'non-contributory' income for Joan. As one back-bencher he knew had cynically said, 'We're under-employed and unappreciated so why not shoulder your way to the trough.... everyone else does!'

Nowadays Davidson felt like a man apart, as if the political mast didn't exist which he could pin his colours to. He couldn't tolerate the way the Lib-Dems were emasculating government policies, the party's continuing irresolute behaviour over Europe, and their preference for favouring the extreme rich, made even more prominent by the savage economies affecting both middle and working class alike. They were well on the way towards years in the political doldrums, he told himself, and the leadership didn't seem to know or care!

Nor was there much comfort for him amongst his regular supporters. A set of them had adopted him, drawn Joan and him into their rarefied social gatherings almost from the onset of his political career. But while he might work assiduously in the House on their behalf when the need arose, he couldn't identify with them. The bulk of the landowners, farmers and businessmen who encircled him most weekends seemed to feel that they'd cornered 'right'. That somehow their privileged lives – born of subsidies, old wealth, tax concessions – gave them sole moral authority. Whether it was the sanctity of the Royal family, the need for an independent nuclear deterrent, the gaoling of troubled alienated teenagers, the comments were invariably predictable with little or no sign of original thought. Was there a huge school in some place where they were habitually indoctrinated?

Davidson's mood eased as he left the A68 and drove towards the beckoning lights of Culwell. Joan knew him, and was the only one. The home would be an oasis of peace and warmth. The excited chatter of the girls at first, and then a light supper with a good bottle of wine. She would know that he needed fortifying after a week in the House, and more imminently there was a sapping round of constituency functions looming this weekend.

Yet again, as he negotiated the Land Rover along the tree-lined red ash of his drive, he thought of what else he might do. But as always the idea was met by the insurmountable wall of an MP's salary, the more than generous expenses, the two directorships that depended on his input whenever agricultural issues were on the Commons agenda. He stopped in front of the large bungalow, swung his legs out of the vehicle and began to smile....

CHAPTER THREE

The scene was one which would have left few untouched. The broad, oval sweep of the village green splashed with the scarlets and blacks of waiting riders. The old coaching inn on one side, the Norman church on the other, and connecting the two a jumble of stone cottages and houses, many with gardens which were still in flower. In the pale, autumnal sunshine it was rural England at its most pleasant.

Archibold Lawrence Driggs sat his chestnut hunter underneath one of the four huge oaks fringing the road which led past the inn. He nodded occasionally, a smile softening his aquiline face, as he recognised and was recognised. Around him the throng of riders, about twenty in total, either sat patiently like him or fought to control the more temperamental of the mounts. 'The indomitables' someone of their number had aptly called them: the much depleted band who had refused to allow idiotic Labour and its rag-tag brigade of lunatic leftists, bleeding hearts and class haters to completely trample hunt traditions into oblivion. The supporters weren't to be pushed around either, and along with the casual onlookers quite a bunch of them were present.

Driggs knew they owed much to their followers. Without them they wouldn't have been able to operate at all in the old way. Often working with the kennel and terrier men, they had become practised in thwarting the activists, blocking bridle paths when the kill approached, disabling vehicles, even physically mixing it with them when the circumstances warranted. Anything to keep the buggers – with their video cameras and mobile phones – away from where the action was coming to a head.

His thoughts were interrupted by the spectacle of Robson trying to subdue his rearing horse. The man and his big-boned, sturdy wife, now in the act of stretching a helping hand to grasp the halter of the excited animal, were both regulars. They ran a firm specialising in agricultural machinery, and with so many landowners and farmers gathered in the same place a double motive could be ascribed for their presence, he cynically reflected.

Alec Ritson was in his line of sight too, in conversation with Dodds, and, as usual, smiling. He had much to smile about, did Ritson. He was a handsome man, blessed with oceans of old money, a prominent member of the local Countryside Alliance, and Driggs couldn't stand him. He sneered as he watched Ritson trot smilingly towards another group. By his lights the man was a phoney, one of the 'soft' rich, someone who when a fox was cornered and the gore started flying was seldom to be seen.

The sound of protesting tyres rather than engine noise reached his ears. He turned and saw a mud-splattered Land Rover slew to a stop in one of the few gaps left by the serried lines of horse-boxes and vehicles. Joe Golightly, the kennel man and sole employee of the Hunt, jumped from it to stride hurriedly across the green. Driggs watched him reach the pack of yapping hounds and look up to engage the stocky figure of Clive Henshaw in conversation.

The men were perhaps thirty yards away, but almost immediately from the expressions and body language he had a good idea of what was being said. Golightly's seemed defensive, as if he was trying to justify his behaviour in circumstances he was unsure of. He kept gesticulating in an almost apologetic manner towards the heavily wooded area which met the village at its southern end. While Henshaw, his square face stern and forbidding, interjected only briefly but apparently very much to the point, judging from Golightly's obvious discomfort.

Driggs knew that demeanour of old. He and Henshaw had clashed a number of times at Hunt meetings and functions. Clash being the operative word, for one couldn't disagree with him without soon engendering a confrontation. The man's innate belligerence would surface and he'd try to browbeat whoever was arguing with him. Driggs grinned to himself. He rather enjoyed baiting the bully; he was particularly fond of obliquely suggesting he might garner support to depose him as Master. Not that he had the slightest interest in the job, of course. He wouldn't be able to abide the petty day-to-day detail. Let Henshaw and his like attend to that – they weren't good for much else. But it was first-rate sport to enrage the man, make him think the position he so cherished was at risk.

And as Henshaw abruptly turned away from Golightly to trot across the green, Driggs saw the scowl on his face disappear to be replaced by the ingratiating smile that was nowadays presented to him. His acid tongue, the facility to leave him red-faced and floundering, had nonplussed the man too often; where he was concerned, and quite against character, Henshaw went to appreciable lengths to preserve civilities.

"A mite chilly for sitting around, Archie," Henshaw said, reining in beside him.

"It certainly is," Drigg said coolly, "The sooner we get riding the better."

The angry look reappeared on Henshaw's face as he caught sight of the kennel man walking back over the green. "Too true...., but if we leave it to that lazy bugger, Golightly, we'll never get started. All he's able to say is he's seen some tracks in Linklater's wood," he snorted. "They're probably weeks old."

"He's the best at the craft I know," Driggs said pointedly. "By God you do go on about nothing. Must you be so consistently obnoxious?"

The adam's apple bobbled at Henshaw's throat, a flush began to suffuse his face; he opened and closed his mouth a couple of times without any words emerging. His thorough discomfort was suddenly relieved by the arrival of Dodds, whose black came mincing towards them in crab-like fashion.

"Morning, Nigel," Driggs called, turning dismissively away from Henshaw.

"Morning gentlemen," Dodds replied, as he pulled his mount to a halt. "It looks like we've got a good day in store for us."

Henshaw grunted, gave Driggs a murderous look and then spurred his horse towards the middle of the green.

"The Master doesn't seem to be in the best of humour this morning," Dodds observed, looking after Henshaw's retreating figure.

Driggs scratched the beak of his nose. "No…, he was," he said, grinning. "But he isn't any more."

Dodds glanced speculatively at the tall, hard-framed man beside him. He seemed so self-possessed, always in control whatever the situation. Driggs intrigued him. He was the only person he knew who could put Henshaw in his place, and judging from the expression on the man's face he had just performed that much-needed service yet again. But there was a dark side to the landowner. Rumour, too persistent to ignore, had it that Driggs was adept at twisting subsidies out of Whitehall. The story Dodds had heard was that Driggs played the role of the bountiful host superbly, wining and lunching the visiting inspectors while his men smartly relocated stock, already tallied, to his neighbouring farm a couple of miles away. Then there was a whisper, just a whisper, that in the last couple of years he'd also become involved in something else; something….

A horn suddenly sounded, three tuneless blasts diverting Dodds and demanding attention.

"Looks as if the Master has decided we're off," Driggs commented.

Henshaw, his ebullience seemingly restored, stood on the stirrups, a whip in one hand and the horn in the other, bellowing orders. Gradually a pattern emerged. With Henshaw continuing to harangue and gesticulate, riders, hounds and supporters eventually segregated and an order emerged. Patch, the lead dog, set off towards the southern end of the village accompanied by the boisterous pack and two flanking riders, and behind them, the hooves resounding on the tarmac road, trotted the main body of the Hunt.

But the procession had hardly left the village when it began to unravel. Driggs' first indication of trouble was the heightened row coming from the pack; then rounding a sharp bend just beyond the last house he saw the reason. An old car was parked on the grass verge, and near it two huntsmen were desperately trying to control their rearing horses. Around them was chaos as the hounds fought over dollops of tinned meat being spooned to them by a pair of long-haired youths. A third, rather dishevelled, individual in a dirty anorak and jeans, was further up the road and intent on maintaining the pandemonium by lobbing generous measures over the hedge into the adjacent field. Clearly the three spoilers hadn't been fooled by the sight of a lone rider leaving a false trail an hour before.

Driggs heard Henshaw's filthy expletive a few yards away from him. Then he too felt the ire rising, and acted. Clenching the reins in a vice-like grip he forced his chestnut through the fighting hounds to slam into the young men. One was hurled into the side of the car, and the other knocked off his feet to end sprawling in the road. Then, pulling his mare's head round, he was spurring it towards the third spoiler with Henshaw and Robson close behind him.

The saboteur saw the danger bearing down on him and began to run. A hound got entangled in his legs; he stumbled, then fell to land on all fours. Driggs reached him and, bending sideways from the saddle, lashed his riding crop across the back of the youth's neck. Then as his momentum carried him past he glanced back to see Henshaw deliver a similar blow.

The young man, howling with pain, regained his feet as his two friends scrambled into the car to make their escape. He looked fearfully at Driggs and Henshaw in the act of turning their horses, at the massed huntsman in the other direction, then plunged through a small gap in the hedge. He tumbled into the field beyond, picked himself up and with one trouser leg rent to the knee raced off, screaming his outrage.

Driggs, patting his mare's head, trotted back. The battered old car, engine stuttering, vanished round the bend towards the village as a small group met him.

"We certainly taught that bloody lot a lesson," Henshaw pronounced triumphantly.

"Wasn't it all a bit excessive?" Alec Ritson said sharply, his splendid smile now conspicuous by its absence. "Whipping, for God's sake, we're not in the Middle Ages! How on earth will the Alliance sanitise this if it gets out?"

Driggs realised the criticism was mainly aimed at him and began to frame a caustic reply, but Henshaw overrode him.

"Absolute bloody rubbish!" he snapped, looking daggers at Ritson. "You can't talk to scum like that."

"They're probably university students," Ritson said, refusing to be intimidated. "But whatever they are, they still don't deserve whipping."

Henshaw shook his riding crop at him. "They're thugs, I tell you. All they understand is a good kick up the arse and the more of it they get the better." He jerked his mount's head around, looking hotly back to see if the pack had reformed. "Anyway we've wasted enough damned time, let's get moving!"

Driggs nudged his mare close to Ritson's. He leaned forward from the saddle, a mirthless smile playing across his face. "Don't get too smart, Alec," he said.

*

It had been Aileen's idea to take advantage of his long-standing interest in photography, and she'd been responsible for the snapshots, pictures of various stalwarts of the Hunt at work, play, going about their lives. An incremental turn of the screw she called it - a mailing of 10 x 6 inch black and white photographs, which, shortly after dropping on their doormats, would be upsetting them further. Under the red light the unprepossessing face of Henshaw swam into Lauder's sight, a shot using the zoom lens of him craning forward into his shop window to reach a cut of meat a customer had selected. The alarm on the stop-clock rang, but watching the tones developing he waited some seconds longer before transferring the photographic paper to the wash tray. He swirled it a few times then raised the tongs to allow surplus water to drain off. Then he carefully immersed the photograph in the fixing solution.

A couple of minutes later Lauder emerged from the breeze-block cubicle in the corner of his garage. He held a rack on which four photographs were pegged - the results of his efforts that morning. There was Mr and Mrs Smith – having a bout of togetherness – jointly pushing an overflowing trolley from a local supermarket. Dodds looking mulishly at an acquaintance he'd met in Hexham market-place, someone whom Lauder didn't recognise but Aileen maintained was a regular, and the incomparable Henshaw, of course.

They were good – no graininess, sharp definition – showing facial imperfections like blemishes, discolouration below the eyes, line and stubble. And with the emphasis decidedly on the black, looked both severe and stark, which was just the effect he wished to convey. Lauder gazed at the photographs with some satisfaction. They weren't in themselves going to be hammer blows. But as Aileen had described, taken in conjunction with what he was doing, they represented another turn of the screw. There would be more photographs following, and it might just be the final straw for a few. The fact that they were being watched during the day in addition to the harassment he was providing, the reason for severing their links with the Hunt.

Lauder put the photographs back in the dark room and then moved to the open garage door. His two-bedroomed, sandstone cottage across the gravel drive was surrounded by fields; and he scanned them looking for any sign of moving figures. The Hunt would be in saddle by now. It was just after eleven on a fine but crisp October morning, and they normally started about an hour earlier. He hadn't seen any of the advance guard yesterday afternoon – Golightly and his odious partner, Kerr, who blocked earths, looked for fresh tracks and generally disturbed the foxes in readiness for their masters to ride. But that didn't mean the Hunt wouldn't put in an appearance. Around him, stretching away to the north and west, almost as far as the eye could see, was semi-moorland, ideal for uninterrupted riding, and, because of the absence of roads, deadly for any fox they might uncover.

He decided to stay outdoors do some weeding in the herbaceous border at the far side of the house. The vantage was even better there, and his attention to the prize specimens starting to dominate the patch long overdue. He shrugged into an old coat, donned a pair of wellingtons, selected the implements he needed and left the garage.

Lauder felt his mood darkening as he hoed. It wasn't that he disliked gardening; rather it was his continuing thoughts of the Hunt which were upsetting him. Saturdays were the worst times. The role he had cast for himself had to be preserved. Unlike the protestors, he couldn't get involved in openly harassing the huntsmen, throwing tit-bits for the hounds. His identity had to remain secret so he could remain free to operate. But with the euphoria of the other night a memory and knowing what might be happening not very far from him, he felt useless, depressed. Had he been kidding himself in thinking his methods – the nocturnal forays, the photographs - would make a difference!

Lauder knew very well that the large contraction in the Hunt membership was not his doing. In fact it was the haemorrhaging which had drawn him back to the struggle. For mere months after the implementation of the Ban some had returned to their old ways and were killing foxes again. According to Kerr, thug and the Hunt's big-mouthed terrier man, he had learned second-hand it had sparked off furious rows within the ranks, with the bulk of the members protesting that no matter how bad the law was they objected to being plunged into criminality. Then, slowly at first, then torrentially, the numbers at meets began falling, with the brighter, the pleasure riders, those no longer conditioned by the traditional dogma, reacting with their feet and debit cards.

And now he was pitted against those who remained – the hard core, some of them so ingrained with violence they were dangerous. Would they, then, be really affected by what he was doing? Did his efforts amount to little more than a pin prick on an elephant's hide? Lauder shook his head, his expression downcast. He set aside the hoe and began to two-handedly transfer the heap of weeds he'd collected into a barrow. Suddenly he stopped midway between the ground and the new pile he was making. The ball he held disintegrated, sending a cascade of weeds and soil onto the lawn, and down the insides of his wellingtons. He swore loudly, doubly irritated. Irritated by his own clumsiness, and irritated by the realisation that he'd allowed circumstances to impair his thinking.

He'd been wholly missing the point, and it was difficult to reconcile since he'd been along that mental path before. The very nature of the extremists within the Hunt was his strength! Unmoved they might be by his present tactics, but they were bound to see them as an escalating process. Addicted to violence themselves, they couldn't think other than that he would eventually use force, that shortly he would be firing barns, swinging a baseball bat.... So there was no need to change his strategy. It would be increasing the psychological pressure for him – rattling the primitives, making them more and more paranoid.

The sound of a hunting horn carried on the wind, and Lauder's smile disappeared as quickly as it had come.

*

The terrain before him was bare and treeless, a series of fields interconnected by a mosaic of grey limestone walls. To the left, about two miles away, perched the hamlet of Denwick, and straight ahead, punctuated only by a solitary farm building, the rising ground began to give way to moorland.

Luck had been on their side. The fox had broken cover and left the heavily wooded area of the valley to run north. Had the animal panicked to flee blindly? Or was its lair somewhere in the uplands and it was on the brink of a vanishing act?

However, as Driggs sped forward in the van of riders he saw the distance between the fox and the clamouring pack was lessening. Henshaw, about fifty yards ahead with Robson and another horseman, plainly thought likewise. The stocky, red-coated figure jumped a wall and then raked his mare's flanks to gain even more speed.

Driggs cleared the wall too, wisely choosing a spot where a number of the uppermost stones had dislodged. The fox was clearly visible now, and it was showing definite signs of wear. An old vixen, its reddish-brown coat threaded with grey the animal was no longer running with the vigour it displayed on breaking cover twenty minutes ago.

The Hunt supporters were sensing the upper hand as well. Away to his right, about four hundred yards off, came shouts of encouragement, a flurry of excited cries. A cart track met a gate there and had become the latest gathering point. Cars were arriving and men jumping from them, hoisting themselves onto walls and gate rungs to get a better view. He spotted Kerr, the terrier man, his muscular frame unmistakable even at that range. They were the regulars – individuals he'd known for years – bristly countrymen with dour faces, the same shabby style of dress. It was amazing the way these people could keep up with the chase; using their knowledge of the tracks and back roads they were often more in touch with the fox, when the kill neared, than quite a number of the huntsmen.

With the tumult coming from the hounds and the uproar to the side of him, the din was deafening. Driggs watched Henshaw angle away from the pack and immediately realised what he was doing. He had to hand it to him – he didn't in the least like the man but he had to grudgingly admit he knew about hunting. Henshaw, experienced campaigner that he was, had decided they must have startled the fox near its lair; and that the beast, now badly tiring, would break for what it believed to be sanctuary in the valley.

The analysis was perfect. Leaning forward on his horse, its hooves sending up clods of earth as it sped over an area of poorly-drained pasture, Driggs saw the fox suddenly turn in a southerly direction. But then it saw the small group of riders closing in on a converging course. The animal tried to accelerate, saw it was going to be intercepted, then frantically twisted back to the line of its original flight.

Driggs spurred his big chestnut. On either side of him riders were shouting, the air filled with the baying of the dogs, as a wave of huntsmen galloped across the field. The gap between the hounds and their quarry had narrowed to a mere twenty yards, and because of Henshaw's pre-emptive move he was now one of those in the lead.

Driggs braced himself as another, even bigger, limestone wall reared up. It was nearly six feet high, and plainly recently tended because there were no breaks to be seen. He knew he wasn't the best of horsemen and jumping wasn't exactly his forte. But the need never arose. The fox made a desperate leap; for a moment it scrabbled at the upper stones, all four legs jabbing the wall to obtain a purchase. One paw found a hole and for a few brief seconds the animal hung, its body near vertical and flattened to the wall. Then it fell backwards to the ground.

The pack fell upon it. No sooner did the old fox recover to turn snarling than the lead dog hurled itself in. Driggs, now thirty yards away and shouting at the top of his lungs, saw it fasten on the fox's flank. The other dogs leapt in.

Until about six, with the rest of the pack a seething mass of ferocity around them, had seized on the animal.

The fox vanished from Driggs' view as he and the others yanked their horses to a stop. Its head fractionally resurfaced, snarling and snapping always too late as yet another wound was inflicted. Then it was hauled down again.

A vivid red spray of arterial blood spurted from the vortex of the pack. It fountained to a height of about three feet, held there for about fifteen seconds, then slowly subsided. There was a cacophony of noise as scarlet-muzzled hounds tore at their victim, even fought savagely amongst themselves to get at the animal.

Henshaw sat on his horse watching the carnage about ten yards away from Driggs and a knot of huntsmen. His feelings of elation and triumph were rapidly ebbing as he saw Ritson and another rider turn away, unable to witness the scene. He snorted contemptuously at their expressions of revulsion, their sudden desire to examine distant skylines. He could to some extent understand the attitude of the few females present. Women were soft, too emotional – basically unsuited for hunting. But these men.... Christ, what a bunch of bloody phoneys they were! They denied what they did, there could be no excuse for them. They were happy enough parading around like characters from Surtees – raising their stirrup cups to onlookers at the start of a meet, galloping across the fields. But when it came to the point of the hunt, the gore and the shit; recognising the dark side which was in each of them, they couldn't carry it through. It made him livid. If they'd had to struggle and prove themselves as he once had they wouldn't be so particular. If they'd had to stand up to a cantankerous, evil-minded father – the old bastard he was – every day in the business, on the farm, then they'd have some backbone. They would understand that when the blood started flying in this life, and it wasn't yours, you'd won, picked the right side. Then you could relax and enjoy because it was in you. These sorry buggers weren't men enough to face up to that; they'd be siding with those bloody spoilers next.

He signalled to Dodds, and he and Robson, along with a couple of others, forced their horses into the cauldron of the pack. The smell of fresh blood hung in the air, frightening the animals, and the huntsmen had to fight with the reins as they pushed the dogs away. A patch of crimson-puddled earth appeared, revealing the fox. The vixen lay crumpled and quivering on its side with blood welling from dozens of wounds. Its coat was saturated, the threads of grey quite visible during the chase now no longer existed. There was a huge gash, pumping blood, travelling from its throat to the back of the neck, and one of its rear legs was almost severed, the limb at an unnatural angle to the flank and held only by a few shredded muscles.

The old animal somehow lofted its head to look at Henshaw and the other huntsmen. The gaze from the light brown eyes was languid, almost trance-like. Time seemed suspended as it looked, the red tongue protruding from the side of the jaw, its breath coming in ragged pants. Then suddenly the fox convulsed, its head smacked the ground and it lay still.

As if just cued, Golightly's Land Rover, with Kerr beside him, came swaying and bumping onto the scene. The vehicle stopped, and Henshaw watched the kennel man smartly emerge to take care of his charges. He first unceremoniously grabbed the fox by its tail then dumped it in the back of the Land Rover, before calling the dogs to him.

"A good fox, Clive" Driggs said, reining in next to him.

Henshaw nodded, his reaction guarded. He was never quite sure where he was with the man. Could this unexpected affability be a ploy to wrong foot him before another attack was mounted!

"Mind you," the farmer said, smiling thinly, "the manner of its demise seems to have rather disturbed some of our drawing room types."

Henshaw's eyes followed the hounds as they went by. A tightly packed group – tail-wagging, pleasant – far removed from the slobbering, savage pack of a few minutes ago. He relaxed, sensing common ground between them.

"They make me sick, Archie…., they really do."

CHAPTER FOUR

Lauder strode out along the lane from his house. It was a cold, starlit evening, and about fifty yards ahead of him he could see the scatter of light coming from the loosely grouped houses in the village. He glanced down at the bunch of flowers he held and smiled to himself. He particularly enjoyed these intimate dinners with Aileen on Saturday nights. They'd settled into a pattern in recent months, preferring to visit cinemas, restaurants, the night club in Newcastle, earlier in the week, when the crush was less and the service therefore better.

He reached the third terraced house in a row of five at the edge of the hamlet and, his pace quickening, walked up the length of the small garden. Aileen, hearing his knock, met him half way into the entrance hall. With a whoop of delight she flung her arms around him and then raised her face to be kissed.

Lauder hugged her. He'd met Aileen ten months ago, shortly after the sale of his insurance brokerage had projected him into an early retirement. And now, gently disentangling himself to look at her, he was once more reminded of just how fortunate he'd been. She was a picture – fair shoulder-length hair framing a serene, oval-shaped face, the eyes now rather archly regarding him a deep blue, and a figure which spoke of ripeness with the soft swell of her pink sweater, the curve of hip from the waistband of her black skirt.

"Now, Mr Lauder," she said in a mock Lancashire accent, "you're not planning on tampering with the help already – the dumplings will be boiling over!"

Lauder burst out laughing and picked up the roses he'd put on the hall table seconds after entering the house.

"These are for the lovely lady," he said grinning.

"Oh Iain, they're gorgeous....thank you," she said, pushing her nose into them, then suddenly purposeful. "Look, why don't you go into the lounge and pour yourself a drink. The meal will be on the table in ten minutes."

"Fine," he replied and, unable to stop himself, lingered momentarily to watch the shapely legs retreating towards the half-open door.

Aileen realised perfectly well what he was about and, with a flounce of her skirt, turned to shoot him a knowing smile before disappearing into the kitchen. Lauder hung up his windcheater and, now reduced to a blue shirt, matching tie and fawn pants, moved into the small lounge. The room, as ever, was pleasant and welcoming. Lamps from two of the walls shed a warm yellow glow; a 'living-coal' effect from the gas fire added to the illumination, and the combined result served to enhance the greens and golds of the carpet, settee and arm chairs. He glanced appreciatively around him as he stood at the drinks cabinet preparing a whisky and soda. With the soft music playing in the background, the aura of comfort, he felt in many respects as much at home here as he did in his own house.

A delicious smell greeted him when he went into the kitchen. Aileen stood at the oven, a stray lock of fair hair falling across her flushed face, as she dealt with the contents of three simmering pans.

She glanced at him, her tone bantering. "If sir would like to open that bottle of wine over there, the menu of diced melon with ginger, hotly followed... I hope... by tagliatelle, will be served shortly."

Lauder's eyes followed hers to the pine table at the end of the big kitchen. He saw the ice-bucket chilling its contents, the candelabra in a central position, a little spray of fresh flowers and two place settings complete with carefully folded serviettes. And once more he was struck by how well and how seemingly effortlessly Aileen did things.

"You might have been a little less slapdash in laying the table," he said provocatively. He could still hear her chuckling when the cork of the Chablis exited with a slight pop.

The light-hearted mood persisted throughout the

candlelit meal. They talked about the holiday they'd arranged in the Canaries after the turn of the year. They touched on Christmas plans when both their sons would be visiting. Lauder told a golfing joke which, with his usual deadpan delivery, had Aileen, a fellow addict, weak with laughter.

But the mood changed abruptly within minutes of them retiring to the lounge. It began with an apparently innocuous question by him. They were sitting side by side on the sofa – Aileen sipping coffee, Lauder chasing his with a brandy, when he said,

"Did you get out today?"

Aileen's face darkened, the full mouth pulled down at the corners. "I think a fox was killed early afternoon," she whispered. "I heard the clamour of the dogs even above the car radio on my way back from the shops. So I stopped, but try as I might I couldn't see anything. You know how the land undulates as it rises towards Harrison's farm...."

Lauder nodded, put his glass down on the coffee table and reached for her hand. He looked at her sympathetically, knowing what she must be feeling.

Aileen struggled with herself for a number of seconds, then with a deep breath continued, "I hung round for a bit. Then sure enough a couple of car loads of those vile supporters, grinning like cheeses, came past. The first of the huntsmen I saw, horse-box and all, was a man called Driggs. He farms west of Matfen, just off the military road."

"How do you know that twerp?"

"I met him at a cocktail party given by Robbie's firm about five years ago."

Lauder didn't say anything. He knew of Robert Coulson, and not only from Aileen – ex-husband, stud of the shires and hot-shot lawyer to the area's landowners.

"I remember thinking there was something cold and unfathomable about Driggs. I didn't like him at all. Then when Robbie was out of earshot he came on rather strong."

"At least it shows the man isn't entirely devoid of decent values."

"Oh, it wasn't that," Aileen cried. "What a simpleton I was. With Robbie in and out of so many beds at the time, he must have thought ours was a marriage of convenience and therefore I was available. I know I complained to Robbie about him later. But he just laughed – said I'd probably misread him, and how he was so awash with money we should cultivate him."

"I'll cultivate him," Lauder said ominously, "but I don't think he'll like it."

Aileen very deliberately put her coffee cup on the table and turned squarely to face him. "I'm not so sure I care for your use of the first person Iain," she said, an edge to her voice. "I thought it was going to be 'we' from now on." She rose, gathered up the two cups and saucers and silently went into the kitchen.

Lauder was relieved for the chance to muster his thoughts. He knew he'd made a gaffe. If he were honest with himself he'd been avoiding the issue, stringing Aileen along, and he could understand her anger. She was every bit as committed as he was. He still remembered the mixture of distaste and contempt on her face, watching the Boxing Day meet in the town square at Corbridge; the smiling riders doing trot-abouts, some brandishing stirrup-cups, touching and raising their hats to the onlookers. The whole awful charade of decent country people, now much reduced in ranks, wanting to cull a pest in the most efficient way possible, yet thwarted by the past legislative victimisation of Blair and his cronies. Her expression of the scene had emboldened him, acted like a beacon, and a little after approaching her – despite the initial guarded reaction of her son, Will – he had discovered she was as like-minded as he.

Aileen returned to the room, holding a glass of wine, and sat down at the other end of the sofa. Lauder looked across the space between them. "I was thinking," he said too brightly, "that we could move towards a more direct involvement of yourself by stepping up the photography angle. I got four away in the post today. It's a good idea – we should milk it; let the core members know through the morning mail that whatever they do, they're being watched."

"You're making a lot of mileage out of this, Iain," Aileen said coolly, "more than it deserves. As a tactic it's relatively low grade – I never saw it as more than an adjunct to the main activities anyway."

"Oh come on, Aileen.... It could prove a real thorn in their sides."

"Don't patronise me, Iain," Aileen said quietly, the force of her feelings only betrayed by the flush moving up from her throat. "I'm not belittling the idea, after all it was mine - just putting it into proportion. But that's not what this is about, is it?"

"I'm not sure what you mean."

"Don't stonewall me, please...I know you too well. What this is about is things are becoming dicier. Shotgun discharges in the night, for example, and therefore it's not for the little woman. That's it, isn't it!"

Lauder grinned self-consciously. "I thought you could build on the photography, and we'd work you into the other gradually."

Aileen bounced her bottom along the settee to end up with an arm around him and her head on his shoulder. "But I want to be involved now, darling," she said, seeking his hand with her free arm. "I'm just as incensed by the barbaric activities of these people as you are. You know that. Also I want to help you because you're mine....So the two reasons together are terribly potent. It would be cruel of you not to involve me."

Lauder looked helplessly at the face smiling sweetly at him. It seemed, reservations or not, he was facing a fait accompli; short of badly hurting Aileen - which was unthinkable- -on his next foray he would have company.

In a couple of respects it would be a good thing. That business at the Smith's a couple of months ago was a case in point. He'd lugged the dead fox – a road kill discovered the day before – across their patio through the pools of light streaming from the windows; he'd been close enough to hear snatches of conversation despite the general babble. It only needed someone at the party to turn their head and he would have been spotted. Then to crown it all he found he'd forgotten the notices. Help, then, if only to remind him in the heat of the moment, would have been invaluable, lessening the risk he ran. Her assistance as driver would be a bonus as well. Fifty-percent of his outings had entailed getting out of the vicinity damned fast once he'd acted. How much easier it would be if he could throw himself into the car and be conveyed away within seconds of his feet hitting the floor. One night, he couldn't help thinking, those extra seconds in finding the keys and starting the engine might badly count against him.

But overwhelmingly against those pluses was a huge minus. Aileen had referred to it without, he was sure, realising the degree. The fact was things were becoming uglier – he'd stirred up the proverbial hornets' nest. The shotgun incident was proof of that. He'd rather glossed over it yesterday on the phone to her, describing Dodds' action as a warning shot. But he hadn't been frank. He knew from the conversation he'd overheard while hidden in the trees, and his reflections since, that the man had intended to harm him. The struggle had entered a new phase – he was thoroughly unsettling them and therefore could expect much, if not more, of the same.

And that got to the kernel of his worries. Were two of them not bound to increase the risk of detection! Alone, he made on the spot decisions in silence; if the circumstances necessitated a change of tack there was no need to communicate with all the attendant danger of being overheard. Then there was the question of mistakes; to be completely realistic with Aileen as his partner the probability didn't just rise by a factor of two. She didn't have his experience of undercover activities; her past hadn't featured a string of NCOs barking and snarling at her. Unlike him, she knew next to nothing about skills such as non-silhouetting practice, or soundless approach, which were so deeply implanted in him they were almost second nature.

"You appreciate you could go to gaol." he said.

"It wouldn't be for long," she replied, smiling angelically, "and we could send one another love letters."

"I doubt if the University would approve of one of their ecology lecturers being the subject of criminal proceedings."

"If I'm pushed out, as you imply," she said unfazed, "then we'll be able to spend more time together...go on holiday whenever we like."

Lauder took a sip of brandy and marvelled yet again at the woman so warmly moulding onto the side of his frame. At fifty-eight and about twelve years her senior, he knew he was lucky. But with it came a pang almost of grief that he'd not met her thirty years ago. She provided such a contrast to what he'd known in his marriage. Born in the late sixties, the only child of two teachers, she could so easily have been ruined. But they were at pains to avoid it, impart the values they espoused. And the outcome was the balanced, affectionate woman now pressing against his shoulder, someone who was so fiercely intolerant of cruelty to children and animals that, at times, she seemingly belied those characteristics. Her philosophy drove her, the idea that with a privileged life came the responsibility to actively challenge wrong whenever there was an opportunity to make a difference.

So he had been without her for a week last summer – she and her group at Harwich checking that the improved export conditions for lambs and cattle were being maintained. There was her work for the PDSA, Save the Children, her involvement in the fight against factory farming....; sometimes he found his head spinning just to keep track.

"No, Iain," she murmured, "don't try to dissuade me. Until we finally convince these hard liners to give up their bestial practices, I want to do all I can to help you. Besides I can't bear it when you're out and I'm left behind. I must go to the window every time I hear a car. I keep thinking something awful has happened to you."

Lauder laughed hollowly. "So now when something awful happens we'll both be in the mire."

Aileen gazed at him, recognising his concern for her. "It won't, darling – you'll see; two of us looking out for one another will reduce the risk. We can discuss things in detail beforehand, and once we go I'll do whatever you decide. You're in charge and there won't be the slightest argument."

"Sounds like the ideal charter for the bedroom." Lauder dryly observed.

Aileen disentangled herself, laughing. "Now young master," she said, mimicking a Lancashire dialect once more, "you're not planning to tek advantage o' the help til pots en pans are cleaned, en kitchen swept."

She rose and, with Lauder grinning behind her, went into the kitchen. There they pitched into a well-honed routine, now an integral part of their Saturday evenings together: he cleared the table and she stacked the dishwasher. Bill, Aileen's handsome golden Labrador, was let in from the out-house, and, to the tune of much tail thumping, received his supper. 'Chum' despatched, a few minutes later they saw him settle in his basket before they returned to the lounge.

"How is Jim, is he well?" Aileen asked, as, with fresh drinks for both of them, Lauder sat down beside her on the settee.

Twenty-eight years old, Jim was one of the few bonuses to emerge from his marriage, which had ended two years ago. A music producer and talented sound engineer, living and working in London, they'd spent a very enjoyable three days with him early in the summer. Lauder could still recall Aileen's face that June night when they ate in the local restaurant. Will, her only son, had been there too, and her expression, at the centre of them, a mixture of pride and intense delight, had barely varied throughout the evening.

"Yes, he's fine and working hard; he says he's really looking forward to seeing us and Will over the Christmas holiday."

Aileen beamed. "They get on famously, those two, don't they? We could pay another visit to that nice restaurant."

Lauder smiled, responding to her enthusiasm. "I can see the kitchen calendar having a number of red rings round those dates."

Only one more allusion was made to the Hunt issue as Aileen sat close to him on the big sofa, legs drawn up beside her. "I'll have a look at the Driggs' place tomorrow afternoon. Take Bill for a bit of exercise, get the lie of the land, and then we'll decide what's to be done."

Aileen nodded. "You'll be careful won't you?"

Lauder looked at her, his expression ironical. "It's purely reconnaissance. I wouldn't dream of making a move now without my trusted lieutenant."

The rest of the evening unfolded in its own usual but magical way. The enchanting creature beside him caressing his face, hands, whispering endearments, the romantic music playing softly in the background. He seemingly plunged into a cloud of intoxicating perfume each time their lips met. The pace of their love-making was slow, unhurried, Her hands sometimes drifting along his thigh, his lightly tracing the contours of throat and breasts through the fine material of her sweater.

They began to dance, swaying to the tempo, their bodies entwined. To Lauder it was as if she completely knew him, knew that at his age he had to be slowly primed. He felt as if he were shedding years as he held her even closer. Suddenly Aileen faltered in mid-step, and with a little gasp lost her time to the rhythm. He didn't look down, neither of them needed to. Aileen flushed, gave him a long heavy look, then, wordlessly, left the room. He heard her begin climbing the stairs.

*

Fred Kerr glanced round the thronged bar of the Turk's Head and then waved a beery hand at his drinking partner, Joe Golightly.

"Henshaw's a right bastard," he said in a broad Geordie accent. "I know, I've run the terriers for him long enough. But, I tell you, he knows hunting and he doesn't piss around."

"So," Golightly replied, looking askance at the coarse face, which, with one eye higher than the other, the splayed nose and red gash of a mouth, was something of an alarming sight.

"What I am saying is," Kerr said, inching his broad shoulders towards his friend, "when we get a line on the bugger – Henshaw's already said as much – we'll do for him!"

"Aye... he's said as much to me."

"And?" the terrier man demanded.

A scowl crossed Golightly's ruddy complexion, hardening the already tough impression created by the lean, angular face, the shaven head. He took a long swallow of beer, belched and wiped his mouth with the back of his hand.

"I'm interested, aren't I," he asserted. "The way things are... subscriptions falling and everything... I won't have a fucking job before long."

Kerr gave a sympathetic grunt and tilted his flat cap up from the top of his forehead.

"Do you ever take that bloody thing off?" Golightly asked, eyeing the checked, sweat-stained object and the few tufts of black hair that had escaped at the front.

Kerr leered at him. "Only for a shag, a bath or both," He downed his almost full pint in one swallow, opening his throat in the way only heavy beer drinkers are practised. "Another?" he said questioningly to Golightly, as he drew a hand across the stubble of his jaw.

"It's my shout, you got the last one."

"Shut it... who's counting? Anyway I'm flush – in a good seam." Kerr said, a self-satisfied grin showing on his face.

Golightly shook his head. "What's different, Fred...you always are!"

As the drinks came Kerr's eyes strayed to the back of the thronged bar. He nodded, acknowledging a white-faced youth who was watching him intently.

"By Christ," he said, his gaze switching to the two terriers sprawled next to the bar stools. "Dave and me had some sport last night. There's a sett not far from the viaduct, and we got this sow out that was built like a fucking ewe," He looked down at the dogs again. "These two and Dave's were getting a right stuffing until I landed it one with the spade. And after that Butch got fastened on its throat, then it was downhill all the way."

Golightly took a drink of his foaming pint. "It's supposed to be illegal, Fred...badger baiting," he said sarcastically. "Has nobody told you that?"

Kerr looked round the packed tap room again, a nasty grin reducing the irregularly placed eyes to slits. "Fox hunting's illegal too, Joe but nobody seems to give a bugger about that," he murmured. He raised the glass to his mouth.

"C'mon – drink up. We'll get some fish and chips in before the rush starts."

Golightly drained his beer. "Lead the way," he replied, getting off the bar stool.

They'd almost reached the door, calling their goodbyes, when Kerr suddenly handed the leash for the terriers to Golightly. "I'll be back in two ticks, Joe... I'm bursting for a piss." He beckoned at the youth he'd earlier recognised and then started pushing his way through the crowd towards the toilets.

A few minutes later the two men left the pub, their shoulders hunched and jacket collars turned up against the chill night air. They hurried down a side street, Golightly still holding the dogs, and emerged in the town square. The Hexham Abbey in all its majesty was bathed in amber light to their left. Ahead, in stark contrast, was an ugly scene, one which was spoiling the peace of the market town all too often nowadays. A group of men, surrounded by a screaming mob, were brawling on the street corner beyond the fish shop.

Kerr's pace quickened. "Hurry up, Joe," he cried excitedly, "we've got a bit of bother here." The crash of a plate glass window disintegrating only seemed to increase his agitation, and reaching the outskirts of the ring he roughly began to push his way through.

Struggling with the dogs and well behind Kerr, Golightly saw the outcome of one of the two fights had already been decided: a demented youth was kicking his blood-splattered opponent, who lay half in and half out of the shattered shop window. The other fight was far more even but nonetheless just as brutal. Two older men, probably in their early thirties, clutched one another by their coats in a ghastly waltz. The dance was punctuated by first one head butting the other in the face, the victim staggering, regaining himself and then responding in exactly the same way. What made it even more horrific was that the fighters, in direct contrast to the baying crowds, apart from a few grunts were each silently locked into the bestial process.

"Fucking well give the bastard it, Ken!" Kerr shouted, recognising the taller of the two as a fellow Turk's Head regular.

Golightly, arriving behind Kerr, reached to tug at his coat. "Keep out of it, Fred, for Christ's sake," he warned, seeing people hurrying away from the vicinity of the fish shop. He knew the owner and knew he would have phoned the police already. "The law will be here any minute."

He'd wasted his words, for suddenly the battle took a new and horrible turn. The smaller one - height was the only distinguishing feature now, so bloody were the messes of their faces - blocked a head butt. Then somehow rearing himself, he brought the top of his forehead down to smash against the other's nose. The unfortunate Ken, his face a scarlet mask, blood spurting from both nostrils, staggered back, then sank to his knees. His opponent moved in, hands free for the first time and clenching into fists, ready to strike the telling blow. But he never made it.

Kerr sprang from the side. The man, so intent on finishing the fight, either didn't see him or reacted too late. For the terrier man momentarily halted, measured the length and delivered a crushing blow to the side of his jaw. The crowd were suddenly silent, even they recognising the mean, disgusting nature of the attack.

The man teetered, valiantly tried to keep his feet, then slumped to the ground on all fours. He shook his head like a dog, eyes glazing, visibly on the edge of unconsciousness. Hampered by the terriers, Golightly started to push through the front ring of the crowd, trying to reach Kerr, knowing what must come. But again it was to no avail.

There was a dull thud as the terrier man viciously kicked his helpless victim in the face. The man keeled over sideways, blood foaming from his ruptured mouth. Then, screeching obscenities, Kerr moved to close quarters, raining kicks to the ribs, the crotch and again to the head.

A police van, siren wailing, blue lights flashing, appeared at the top of the road just as Golightly and the blood splattered Ken got to Kerr. They dragged him away from the stricken man, each locking onto either of his arms.

"For fuck's sake,....Fred!" Golightly exploded, his lean face incredulous, "Were you planning on killing him?"

Kerr violently shook off their arms. He glanced at the police vehicle, now slewing to a halt, the people running and hurrying away, and then sprinted for a nearby alley. The others hesitated a moment, then they took to their heels...

CHAPTER FIVE

Lauder was being propelled along. Bill, with the elastic leash at full stretch, was ten yards ahead of him, thoroughly enjoying himself and setting a brisk pace along the faintly worn path. Away to the right, partially obscured by a hawthorn hedge across a large field, was the farmhouse belonging to Driggs.

Praise be to the previous government and the commitment of the County Council, he thought as he reeled Bill in a little. Not too many years ago a Sunday afternoon walk of the sort he was taking would have been more stressful than peaceful; the possibility always present of being challenged by whoever owned or farmed the land. But now those at the County seat in Morpeth, assiduously supported by the Ramblers Association, had conferred legal respectability. The wide open spaces of Northumberland were criss-crossed with designated trails such as the one he was using; redundant bridle path, ploughed over rights of way, had been rescued, each signposted with the direction and length of route. Some of the farmers couldn't accustom themselves to it though. Only a few months ago he'd watched with some amusement one of the local worthies trying to wrench a sign out of the ground. The man had tugged and heaved for a number of minutes before, red faced and cursing, privately admitting the quality of the installation was too much for him. It seemed the right to roam was another area where old habits refused to die!

But as far as he was concerned, a bogus walker (he only saw the need to cross sizeable tracts of land when jogging or playing golf), what the path gave was anonymity. The chance to inspect Driggs' lair without drawing attention to himself. So he'd parked the car in a lay-by close to the start of the trail, and waited. He was there five minutes, and sure enough a couple of ramblers, complete with rucksacks and sticks, had arrived, given him a cheery wave and set off along the path. He'd waited another two minutes, released the hyper-excited Bill from the car, then began to follow them. To all appearances he was just one of the people enjoying a walk this dry, chilly October afternoon, Even if anyone was watching from the farm, trying to identify a source of potential trouble, there was nothing about him to arouse suspicion. All they would see was a middle-aged man in a flat cap, wearing the ubiquitous green Barbour coat, in the process of exercising his dog.

Lauder walked parallel to a bare hawthorn hedge; about five feet high it was the easterly boundary to the huge field in which the farm stood. He came to a dry stone wall with a stile set in it, which Bill had just cleared in one exuberant leap. A small placard fixed to the wood showing a yellow arrowhead against a dark background confirmed he hadn't strayed from the trail. To his right the wall intersected the hedge before snaking on westwards past the rear of the farm. The corner created seemed a good spot to watch the place unseen.

He ducked low and moved the few paces to the hiding place. Bill answered his call, and after a few licks of his face plus the usual tail thumping, settled down beside him. It was even better than he first gauged; he couldn't be seen by anyone on the main road or coming from it, and the relentless assault of the hedge on the wall had dislodged some of the uppermost stones. He found he could sit, with Bill waiting patiently at his side, and have an unobstructed view of the farm.

It was a big house; conventional shape, roofed in dark blue slate and built of sandstone. The number of windows upstairs on the side he was facing suggested it would run to about six bedrooms. The gable end, looking to the north and the military road, was only relieved by a porch and clearly constituted the main entrance. Outside there was a tarmac circle from which stretched the black-ribbon of the drive, wending towards the road.

Lauder took a small pair of binoculars from his coat

pocket; with the sun behind him he knew there was no chance of reflected light revealing his position. He began to examine the barns at the rear of the house. There were two of them, their light grey corrugated construction in keeping with the stonework of the main building. He realised it was exclusively a sheep farm; while the field in front of him showed innumerable specimens there was no sign of other types of stock. So the barns would be mainly used for storage – winter feed such as hay, plus the housing of farm machinery. Were they home for any working animals though – much like his friend, Bill sitting dutifully beside him? But, search as he might, there were no farm dogs to be seen.

The Land Rover standing at the head of the drive, and parked alongside a dark green Mercedes, took his attention, He studied it for a moment and then lowered the glasses, his expression reflective. Short of a family pet, Driggs didn't need a dog, he reasoned. That sort of four-by-four hi-tech monster he'd seen advertised on television. It would save hundreds of pounds of 'Pedigree Chum' each year because it could negotiate rough and waterlogged terrain and travel faster than a collie. The farmer close to him at home was a great exponent of the new and burgeoning practice. Not for him the whistle and the crook. He was beeping his horn from morning till dusk, and driving his sheep from all manner of difficult places with seemingly consummate ease.

Then there was the question of security lights. Lauder raised the binoculars again to focus on the three lamps; one was above the porch and the other two, equidistant from it, near the corners of the gable wall. He'd encountered something similar last winter when he paid an uninvited visit to the property of the pro-hunting local MP. They worked by detecting movement. But how did the Driggs prevent wandering sheep triggering the lights every few minutes during the night? He scanned the area even more closely…Aah, money – it provided an answer to most difficulties. There was a livestock grid running the full periphery of the tarmac apron at the front of the house.

Lauder rose to his feet, the germ of an idea beginning to take place in his mind. Bill bounded up at him trying to lick his face, happy the inactivity was over, then tail thrashing launched himself forward. Once more under propulsion, Lauder decided he would continue for another twenty minutes. It would produce a much needed release of the dog's surplus energy, and he'd have the opportunity to assemble his thoughts.

Thirty yards into the resumption of the walk, Lauder stopped suddenly, almost garrotting the hapless Bill. He stood gazing unseeingly into the distance, amazed at himself, staggered as to how he'd so unconsciously slipped into a dual mental process. He had been thinking for both of them in that the plan, however unformed, depended on Aileen too. He grimaced – he'd botched dissuading her from becoming involved, but that didn't mean his reservations were any less real. He knew they only had to make one mistake and the consequences would be both swift and very painful.

He began walking again, too preoccupied to notice Bill looking back at him in an uncertain fashion. Whatever they did, he decided, Aileen's part in it had to be marginal. He would be damned rather than expose her to any appreciable risk, He'd best confine her to the driving, and a role which didn't entail her leaving the car. He could build around that; his idea was still raw – needed fleshing out. He would have another look at the turning circle in front of the house on the return leg….

*

Archibold Alistair Driggs sat at his big, leather-topped desk overlooking the fields east on his farm. He pushed away the papers in front of him, feeling a stab of indigestion. Perhaps he had overeaten. Jennie had prepared and served yet another first rate lunch: a tasty lentil soup followed by roast beef, Yorkshire pudding and two vegetables, then blackberry pie and cream to finish with, before making her way outside to be picked up by that feckless husband of hers. Along with Edith – nice, accommodating lass that she was – she also kept the house scrupulously clean, causing him to wonder quite often just what use his wife was. He supposed he would have got rid of Vera a long time ago but for the punitive costs of a divorce. The thought of making a large settlement or worse, relinquishing half of what he owned, was too horrendous to contemplate. So he put up with her, and if he were honest it wasn't too bad. She was an unobtrusive, quiet woman – almost like a ghost about the place. She had her golf and charity work, didn't make demands or question him, and could take a good slagging with little or no fuss.

He saw another figure beyond the hedge walking along the path. Confounded ramblers, no wonder he was suffering from indigestion. They traipsed along at seemingly five minute intervals, interrupting a view which a few years ago was one of empty, rolling countryside in all its glory. Driggs suddenly smiled sardonically. Perhaps one of them was this phantom whom Henshaw and Dodds were so agitated over, spying out the land for another strike. The latter had been bleating to him after the meet yesterday; he hadn't realised that his earlier pleasantries had been to discomfort that cretin, Henshaw, rather than any regard for him. Dodds had gone on about how it was incumbent on them all to be hyper-vigilant because no-one knew where the man would materialise next, saying the same thing several times in different ways. He'd stood his whining for a minute or so, then rounded on him. He grinned at the memory. Dodds had appeared as if hit by a sledgehammer when he told him to stop behaving like "a bloody wet week", and how you couldn't sit around "vaporising like a woman" about what might happen. What counted was what you did when it happened – you didn't "fanny around" like he had, you put "a couple of rounds up the intruder's arse".

Dodds had done a Henshaw, turned an unhealthy colour while his Adam's apple developed a life of its own, then, spluttering something about how he'd never known such incivility, stalked off. Driggs brushed the hook of his nose, the aquiline face hardening. Well, politeness was for anyone but him. His house-master had been polite when he told him at nine years old that his mother had just died. His father had been polite several times afterwards; asking him to stay at school over the holidays, the reasons ranging from absences abroad to fiction about lack of room because of house guests. He mistrusted the trait; whether the subject or the object, it didn't get you anywhere, and invariably led to disadvantage. You didn't get a ripe, young housemaid sitting on your lap by being courteous. You didn't make the likes of Kerr understand you'd brook no deviation to your instructions by being other than confrontational.

His hand smoothed down a few hairs in the greying, well-tended thatch as he glanced around the luxurious room. No.., you had to implant a certain idea of yourself in people's minds – make them realise you were a force to be reckoned with, someone who couldn't be ignored. That was how there was a Bruegel landscape on the far wall, worth four times the amount he'd paid for it at Christie's three years ago. Driggs lit up a large cigar, exhaled and then looked down at the quotation on his desk. That was how, when he replaced the Cessna, he would have a state of the art, two seater jet in the hangar at Newcastle Airport. Golf maestros, film stars, business tycoons got them in their different ways... and he had his...!

*

Aileen glanced searchingly at Lauder above the rim of her tea cup. He'd returned about half an hour ago, and she had pointedly limited her questions until they finished eating. Bill had eaten too and was now gently snoring in the corner of the kitchen.

"How does it look then?"

Lauder eased himself in his chair. "Typical construction for a Northumbrian farmhouse – sandstone and Lakeland slate, big though, one of the largest I've seen. Along with the barns, the farm has a solid, prosperous look to it."

"Yes, our Mr Driggs is by no means short. He owns the farm on the south side too."

Lauder nodded, his expression pensive. "He certainly seems to lack for nothing materially. There was a top of the range Mercedes, almost brand new, leaving the farm when I finished my walk. Then, less exotic, but more relevant to us, he has an expensive lighting scheme for the area in front of the house. There are three lamps and I think they must be activated by movement sensors."

"That doesn't sound good." Aileen said, frowning.

"No it doesn't at first," Lauder replied. He picked up the teapot and poured himself another cup. "You know I normally drink coffee, but when Sunday afternoon tea arrives I can drink oceans of this stuff." He took a drink and looked at her contentedly.

Aileen studied him for a moment, then laughed. "Iain, I believe you're teasing me. That qualification, 'at first' is telling. You're onto something, aren't you!"

Lauder grinned at her and then suddenly became serious. "Well, with a suitable diversion, which I thought you could provide, Driggs' strength could become his weakness."

"I don't understand," she said, "but I sense it's different to what you've been doing – you're breaking new ground."

"You're right there," he replied. "Broadly, what I'm thinking is to disturb Mr Driggs' slumber. Lure him out – pyjamas, dressing gown, livid face and all – enabling me to get inside."

"My God, Iain, this sounds dangerous."

"With a bit of luck it won't be," he said. "Let me explain. The approach to the house is open, featureless.

The drive is about a quarter of a mile long, bisecting a large heavily-grazed field, and the only trees are on either side of the entrance from the main road. There's no gate, just a couple of stone pillars flanking an animal grid.

"Go on." Aileen said, her concentration almost palpable.

"I can't go in that way – I'd be exposed for too long. I'll have to take the shorter route from the side, starting at a point on the bridle path. Then, once in place, tucked in alongside the house, I visualise you coming in. You'd drive up, loud music blaring, and activate the lights by waltzing round the turning circle a few times. Then you'd turn tail and get smartly out of there."

"That's the diversion." Aileen said, wide-eyed.

"Exactly. What I imagine is that Driggs will plunge out of the front door, threatening blue murder, scrabbling with his dressing gown, and make a beeline for the bastard who's upset the house and his sleep."

"And you waiting in the shadows next to the porch," Aileen added, "will get through the door behind him."

"That's it. Mrs Driggs had considerately put two potted firs on either side of the porch, so I should be reasonably hidden until I need to move."

"What then though, Iain?" Aileen asked anxiously. "What happens when you're inside the house?"

"I'll dive into the first thing that provides cover. A stair cupboard, an alcove – whatever; it's quite possible a house of that size will have a cloakroom just off the hall."

"But there could be other people there besides the Driggs," Aileen said, her anxiety no less diminished. "And what about dogs?"

Lauder shook his head. "I'm pretty sure there are no dogs. Coming back this afternoon I let Bill loose for five minutes. You know what a racket he makes when you're throwing a stick for him – he's such a big happy dog. I wouldn't have been surprised if they heard him in Corbridge, yet there was no reaction from the farm."

"Mrs Driggs then... members of the family," Aileen's

tone was urgent. "You could get into the house and find yourself confronted by two or three of them."

Lauder again shook his head. "You know I saw Alan Pickersgill this morning."

Aileen nodded. "He came to measure up for those extra bookshelves you want in the study."

"That's right. Well he's a good joiner is Alan, but he can't stop talking, so much so he borders on the indiscreet. Anyway, I gave him a coffee, gently nudged the conversation round to Driggs and sat back. He's done work for him, and I thought he would never stop. I got everything from his family circumstances to his activities as an intrepid aviator."

"He's got an aeroplane too!" Aileen exclaimed. "My word, I knew he was well-heeled but I didn't realise how… Seems strange, doesn't it – even with two big sheep farms and the ever bountiful EEC you wouldn't think they'd run to such a lavish lifestyle! There must be old money too."

"Perhaps," Lauder said, his voice sceptical. "I wonder, I just wonder…"

But Aileen's misgivings had surfaced again, too insistent for her to contain. "What were you going to say about offspring, Iain?"

"There are two. But they're both grown-up, married and living away from home; the daughter's in Tynemouth and the son, Manchester, I think."

Aileen was still unappeased. "You could run into Mrs Driggs half way down the stairs. You might end up caught between her screaming the place down and Driggs running back with a shotgun."

"I don't think so," Lauder grinned. "Think about it, flower. What would I have done last night if an intruder had come into the house?"

A flush moved up from Aileen's throat and she smiled almost shyly. "You would have told me to stay in bed, and you would have gone downstairs with the baseball bat."

"Precisely," Lauder said, laughing. "It's a macho

reaction, a primeval instinct – the desire to protect the woman, hearth and home against all invaders. Men can't help responding, and women enjoy the feeling of being protected, looked after. I hear Driggs' marriage isn't too rosy, but even he wouldn't kick his wife out of bed to investigate."

Aileen began to visibly relax. "You seem to have thought everything through," she said. "And what happens when you've secreted yourself inside?"

"I wait until the house settles down again and they get off to bye-byes. Then I'll leave notices all over the downstairs – in the toilet, the reception rooms, the kitchen, I've thought of a couple of really offensive points I could make."

Aileen's eyes were gleaming now as she gazed at Lauder. "What a scheme," she enthused. "Wow! What a psychological bomb to toss first to the Driggs and then the rest of them!"

"And we can increase its impact even more if we choose the right conditions."

"How do you mean?"

Lauder didn't answer directly. "Did you see the weather forecast this weekend?" he asked.

"Yes," Aileen replied, looking somewhat puzzled, "the dry spell's ending tonight. There's a big depression coming in from the west – wind and rain, and plenty of it."

"That's good."

"Which bit is?"

"The wind and the rain," Lauder replied. "When I finish at the farm I'll leave all the doors and windows open. I'm afraid the Driggs won't have a very pleasant reawakening either. They'll think they've got banshees in the house, and with a bit of luck I could usher in a few sheep too."

"This is a large step forward, Iain," Aileen said, the excitement bubbling in her tone. "You're making a new statement here."

"I've been thinking the same," Lauder agreed.

"You're saying," Aileen added, "I've thoroughly aggravated all of you up till now, even made some of you afraid, and you haven't been able to stop me. But now the exterior phase is over – the screw is being turned up another ratchet. I'm coming into your homes and you're still powerless to stop me…"

She tailed off, her eyes alive with delight. "It's beautiful," she said, "should work, and will shock them rigid!"

Lauder nodded. The difficulty remained though, just as before, that there would be no way of gauging how successful they were. He necessarily gave hunts-people and their followers a wide berth, publicly paid no attention to their activities whatsoever. He even acquired information about them in the most circumspect of manners, noting registrations as he motored past a meet, scanning the local paper for photographs and articles, and, like today's reconnoitre, going to appreciable lengths to stay unnoticed. For to show undue interest, even make indirect enquiries, with the Hunt in their current paranoid state, would ultimately mean detection and the whole thing crashing down on his head. A number of years ago, before the ban, he reviled them whenever they were in his vicinity – casting doubt on their lineage, referring to them as subhuman; even suggesting, to the wrath of one red-coated individual, that he and his friends might wish to pursue the local children during the school holidays. But now no longer. He was overtly neutral, an apparent fixture on the fence. If an argument broke out amongst his friends he took a back seat, was sickeningly equivocal. Anything rather than draw attention to himself. So when it came to assessing defections, he was guessing the extent of the mayhem he was causing. He was reduced to isolated comments, estimates of turnout on meet days and such subtle signals as the Hunt neither giving contact names nor telephone numbers in its recent press releases. None of which, even collectively, was able to give him anything like an accurate picture.

"A penny for them," Aileen said.

"Oh, I was just thinking – we know we're having an effect on them but we can't know how much."

"We've simply got to keep ploughing on until we sicken the hardcore so much they give up. What we do know is we haven't got a great deal of time. This fascist government," she said angrily. "invariably acting against the people while protecting the rich and powerful, are going to repeal the Act."

Lauder grimaced and nodded.

"But with the League Against Cruel Sports offering rewards for evidence against the Hunt, the spoilers a continuing thorn in their sides, our own form of pressure could tip the balance – be the proverbial hair that breaks...."

"I've never believed that line anyway." he interrupted, looking at her fondly.

"Which line is that?"

"About a prophet not being appreciated in her own land."

For once Aileen didn't react to his banter. "You've put the wind up them, Iain – got them on the run," she said seriously. "I don't think you realise how good a job you're doing."

"And that makes it all the more risky," he said darkly.

Aileen didn't dwell on the inference. "Well, we must be doubly careful," she said quickly, the emphasis on the plural quite perceptible. "Now, how will I know when to drive in?"

"We could prearrange a time which would allow for me getting into place. Or I could phone you on my mobile. We can decide on the night."

Aileen rose and began to place the cups and plates on a tray. She bent and kissed him on the lips.

"Which will be when, lord and master?"

Lauder grinned. "Tomorrow night, I think."

*

Aileen stood at the window and watched Lauder walk down the garden path. He undid the latch on the gate, closed it and, not realising he was observed, strode briskly away. She smiled to herself; each time she saw him in an everyday setting she experienced the same warm sensation, an amalgam of pride and attraction. He was striking, was her man; the tall figure, the upright bearing which, coupled with the pleasant but slightly ironic expression he normally wore, gave the impression of both vitality and intelligence. But it was the eyes in the strong rectangular face which were his best feature: a light almost translucent blue, they seemed to eat into her every time she looked at him.

Her mind was still buzzing from the conversation with him over tea. The intelligence had shown then. She was amazed by the audacity of his plan and its uncluttered simplicity. It seemed yet another example, the cleverest so far, of his ability to wrong-foot and harry the Hunt whenever he moved against them. But above all it was evidence of his commitment to the struggle. She'd never met anyone before who, in striving for what they believed was right, was so single-minded.

He'd talked to her on a couple of occasions about his formative years. How he'd been born into a poor family living in a village on the south side of the Tyne. How his father, a council gardener – twice decorated during the Normandy offensive of 1944 – had struggled during the mid-fifties to properly clothe and feed him and his sister. He spoke of the family's sense of injustice that despite the father's heroism and the sacrifices of other ex-servicemen, life for them and ordinary people remained hard and unchanged. Then, belatedly, a widespread improvement in the early sixties with Macmillan's government relaxing credit, and he, the only one of a class of forty winning a place at grammar school. How, conscious of the tremendous opportunity, he'd worked unstintingly hard and made good progress. Then, at eighteen, upturning it all – Aileen could still remember the scathing tone of his self-criticism – because of a huge mistake. Perhaps motivated by a half-recognised desire to emulate his father, his appetite for study blunted by two demanding years in the sixth form, and certainly fuelled by media accounts of IRA atrocities, he'd idiotically – his own words – opted for military service in Northern Ireland. There followed three awful bloody years in the province, Iain's sole comment on the experience. With a much altered young man emerging: someone determined to never commit physical violence again, and intervene whenever he could to prevent it in others.

And, if anything, he'd confided, that outlook had heightened throughout his adult life. Drawn into the arena of animal welfare in his late twenties – doing voluntary work for one of the main protection bodies, helping fund sanctuaries – he found the abuse gargantuan, a scandal in a country that were alleged animal lovers. It had focused him even more, the constraints on his time made by family and career, the sheer scale of the problem, spurring him to be as effective as possible. And now that resolve was beginning to tell in what they both regarded as the most sustained and iniquitous persecution of dumb animals in modern times.

Aileen, the tray still in her hands, turned away from the window. She walked into the kitchen and began stacking the dishwasher. As she worked she glanced at the overhead clock, registering that in about two hours Iain would be returning for her. They intended to dine in Newcastle that night; the restaurant was Spanish and unusual in having a small dance floor. She'd wear that slinky black dress, she decided, her mood lightening.

CHAPTER SIX

Lauder watched his granddaughter skip to the door holding her mother's hand.

"Say cheerio to Granddad, and give him a kiss," the four year old was instructed.

He knelt down beside the flaxen-haired little girl and pulled her to him. It was curious, he thought yet again, how his daughter gave orders to Rachel concerning him as if he were mentally retarded or suffering from senility. He looked at the cornflower blue eyes, the pink cheeks and the rosebud of a mouth already pursing to plant a kiss on his nose.

"Will you come and see us soon, Grandad?"

"I will."

"And we can play that water game again?" she asked, her eyes sparkling. Rachel and he had spent part of the afternoon splashing one another, by taking turns to throw a tennis ball into a large puddle. It was difficult to say who had the most fun, he or the child.

"Grandad will have to wear his rain coat next time, you got him so wet."

Lauder glanced at his daughter. She was a large version of Rachel, but the loveliness contained, as if a very efficient thermostat was in control. He recognised the code. What she meant was that the game was too wild, that Rachel's red leggings and coat had to be dried in front of the fire afterwards. The little girl's squeals of delight didn't count, nor the heightened facial colour which only cold fresh air can produce.

"Thanks for coming round, Jane," he said, leaning forward to peck her on the cheek.

"It was nice to see you, Dad," she replied. "Do you want to join us for lunch this weekend?"

"There's something buzzing at the back of my mind. So I'll come back to you on that one."

Lauder walked over to the BMW and stood clowning in

front of Rachel while Jane strapped her into the child seat. Then smoothing her skirt as she seated herself in the car, she gave him a perfunctory wave and drove off up the drive.

He watched them go, raising his hand to Rachel as she twisted in the seat to catch a last look at him. That concludes another 'state' visit, he thought, returning indoors. The next 'rodding-through' wouldn't be for another two weeks. He sometimes had Aileen helpless with laughter in using such terms to describe his daughter's fortnightly visits. It was a good safety valve under the circumstances. For while Aileen had never mentioned it, Jane's attitude towards her, on the few occasions they'd met, had barely been polite.

So far Lauder hadn't broached the subject with his daughter, reasoning that given time things would change. But now with no sign of thaw he was beginning to severely resent Jane's attitude. After all, she was the self-appointed custodian of his welfare, appearing regularly to ensure, he suspected, he hadn't descended to the level of a primitive. This entailed her 'jackbooting' through the house inspecting his clothes, the food in the refrigerator, scrutinising lavatory pans and generally locating dirt wherever it might reveal its ugly presence. Despite his dark humour, Lauder knew he benefited from her visits, that Jane's motives were sound. She wrote uncompromising notes to Mrs Walton – who cleaned for him two days a week. Notes he wouldn't dare write himself. After one of her forays he would a couple of days later come home and find in the porch oranges, apples, tinned food, some pre-cooked curries. Whatever he'd been planning to replace, and not yet got round to.

Which made her attitude to Aileen all the more bewildering. For someone concerned for his well-being as Jane, why could she not accept that Aileen was central to his happiness? That he would rather she forgot about all the things she regularly did for him in exchange for a single invitation to lunch for her.

Lauder scratched his head as he sat in the lounge, watching another rain squall developing. He couldn't fathom it. Perhaps it was the contrast between Susan, his ex-wife, and Aileen. Susan, on the one hand, at least as far back as he could remember, was restrained and cool in her manner. While Aileen, on the other, was demonstrative and alive – forever publicly or privately showing him in some way she cared. Perhaps Jane, her mother's daughter in many ways, saw it as effusiveness and mistrusted her, not realising he was the sole object of such warmth. His daughter wouldn't appreciate the extent to which he'd found Susan judgemental, invariably conveying the impression he fell short of her standards. They were close, the two of them – saw one another frequently - and from what he could gather, maddening though it was, his successor was now an accepted and integral part of that side of the family.

When Lauder thought about his marriage he saw that he and Susan had forgotten how to relate to one another. He'd built his career, pursued his concerns in animal welfare, and she'd raised the children. Apart from the odd dinner, her input to his business had been minimal, and if he were honest his contribution as a father hadn't been much more. There'd been family holidays, of course, the occasional disciplinary problem where his intervention was needed. But in the main it was Susan who repaired their emotional difficulties, helped with homework, fed, clothed and nursed them. Their marriage had polarised, and with the inertia came increasing resentment – hers at his part-time activities as father and husband, his at her perception that the limited time he spent in the home was somehow deliberate.

Then when university took Jane and Jim away the harsh fact was that any common ground they'd had disappeared. Not that they'd accepted the situation initially. They both rallied, struggled against it, tried to inject some warmth into the sterility which lay between them. But their values were too different, their philosophies at odds. She couldn't understand how at times he would act, despite being opposed. While he found her too detached from issues which affected him, too inhibited by convention. So with the kids no longer providing a buffer, the friction deepened and the rows multiplied. And with them dwindled the normal compensations of marriage, particularly sex. If anything the act began to accelerate the disintegration of their relationship rather than arresting it. In the last months, on the few occasions they had intercourse, Lauder was left in no doubt that his motives were considered entirely basic, that how he behaved in the bedroom was seen largely as a means of relieving himself.

It had been a release in the end when one night he'd come home and found a note waiting for him in a deserted house. Susan had proved to be the courageous one. She'd seen the cancerous material which made up the mould of their marriage, and smashed it. He knew his successor slightly. Susan had done rather well – the fellow was a prosperous Newcastle businessman in his early fifties, who had lost his wife a year earlier. How they'd met he had no idea. But then Susan's world of bridge nights, golf functions and visits to the theatre with friends had become increasingly a closed book as their lives diverged.

For Lauder it was the turning point. He was very sad for a while. Sad that because of his apparent rigidity he'd lost the classy, elegant woman who had shared most of his adult life. But then he began to rationalise his thoughts, slough off the feelings of guilt. Such perceptions as, if he'd only compromised more, the relationship might have survived, he saw were erroneous. For the truth was that he and Susan had never been suited. It had been masked, of course, particularly in the early days, when their intense sexuality effectively papered over the cracks. But he could remember rarely broaching certain topics or opinions with her. There was a list – some of the items important to him – which once aired would guarantee them arguing furiously.

The loneliness was grim. He learned it was preferable

to have someone, if only to greet and exchange comments about the weather, than no-one at all. He rattled about the big house which had been too large even for Susan and himself, then realising it was part of the problem, brought in an estate agent. With five bedrooms and nearly as many toilets and bathrooms, the house soon sold, and with divorce papers by then in circulation, he sent Susan a cheque for fifty percent of the proceeds. Then he bought another – the house where he was now; it was a third of the former size and, perversely, because of its isolation immediately made him feel more comfortable.

By then change had become endemic for Lauder. It had gathered a momentum which saw him re-evaluating everything he looked at. He began to raise questions about his business life, asking himself just what he was doing and why? The answers – those that came – weren't reassuring, and a few downright disturbing. He took a break in Tenerife, thinking distance would make him more objective. He swam, walked, read and got drunk a couple of times. Then he came back and sold his business.

The disposal of the insurance brokerage proved the last cerebral plank in his rehabilitation. As the benefits of his new lifestyle began to emerge, with them came amazement. Amazement at the huge world which existed beyond the financial one. He joined a local history association, re-ignited his interest in photography, learned gardening was a delight rather than a penance, and began to read extensively. Now, more than a year into retirement, he could barely credit how he'd thought his narrow, structured business life satisfactory.

Lauder began collecting Rachel's toys. He put them in a big box and carried it into the spare bedroom. He decided he would watch the early evening news next. Then a light meal before meeting Aileen, and squaring up to the agenda in hand.

*

The car swayed slightly as another gust of wind caught it. Lauder listened to the sound of rain on the roof, no longer the drum of ten minutes ago.

"It seems to be lessening," he observed.

Aileen nodded. "I should think so. It's been throwing down for almost three hours now."

Lauder squinted through the streaked side window at the black outline of the farmhouse across the fields. He then glanced at his watch. It was ten minutes after midnight, and they'd seen the last of the lights extinguish at the Driggs' home about twenty minutes ago.

"I'll move in a few minutes. Then allow another ten and I should be in place."

Aileen shielded her eyes against the glare of undipped headlights as a fast-moving car approached them. It passed by the lay-by in a cloud of spray, and with the engine sound rapidly receding disappeared towards Newcastle.

"You'll phone me though to confirm?"

"Yes I will," Lauder answered, "and then you come in with your decibels blaring." He caught the white flash of her smile despite the dimness of the car.

"Well, I don't think your terminology is scientifically accurate but I get the gist of what you're saying.... Is there anything else?"

"Don't hang around," Lauder said. "As soon as you see room lights coming on, doors being thrown open – get out quickly."

He paused for a moment, then turned to look at her. "I think you should then go home and wait a while before returning for me."

"All right," Aileen said levelly. "You think that's better than my remaining in the vicinity?"

"I do," Lauder asserted. "After twelve-thirty, certainly weekdays, the police think everybody should be in bed. So they assume every parked car they see either belongs to a burglar or a sex maniac, and start investigating."

"I'll pick you up here then," Aileen replied, "about one-fifteen."

"Clever girl," Lauder said, and giving her a peck on the cheek opened the car door.

Aileen suddenly lunged towards him, plucking at the material of the arm of his coat. "Iain," she said anxiously. "You'll be careful, won't you – you won't take any unnecessary risks?"

"Don't worry," Lauder said with a heartiness he didn't feel. "I'll be alright." He grinned at her, pulled on a ski-mask and got out of the car.

His feet squelched on the sodden earth as he retraced his Sunday afternoon walk along the bridle path. The rain was just a cold drizzle now, carried on a blustery wind from the east. But the deluge earlier had made a big impact. There were pools everywhere, fledgling streams following the lie of the land, and he would have to be careful where he put his feet when he got close to the house.

As for being spotted on his approach, the risk was practically non-existent. With a low, almost unbroken cloud base blocking out all but fleeting glimpses of a quarter moon, the night was so dark he could barely pick out objects a few yards in front of him. A jet passed unseen above him, heading east for the airport, the only indication of its presence the steady throb of engines throttled-down for landing.

Lauder found a break in the path-side hedge, and then very gingerly climbed over the barbed wire fence beyond it. He set off across the field, angling towards the black mass of the farmhouse. Suddenly four or five large shapes reared from their haunches in front of him, and bleating and coughing their protests lumbered off into the night.

His pace dropped to a crawl. He would have to be careful not to disturb the sheep again, he thought, his heart beating faster. The drenched animals were all round him, huddled together for protection against the biting wind. Noise was the problem in these conditions, he told himself, and winced as his right foot descended into a large puddle with what seemed a resounding splash.

The dark forms of the Mercedes and Land Rover were standing in front of the house. He saw they were parked on the flanks of the tarmac apron, tucked up to its perimeter. That was fine – Aileen coming off the drive would be able to swing round in one manoeuvre and then leave quickly. As to the other consideration uppermost in his mind, he was by no means as sure.

Now pressed up against the wall at the corner of the house, Lauder glanced nervously upwards. Although he couldn't see it there was a lamp on the eave almost directly above him, with another two further across the gable wall. He knew they were activated by movement sensors. The question was, how were they aligned? Logic told him that the outer limit of the sensor field would be the livestock grid running along the edge of the turning area. But close to the house was more imponderable. Were the sensors able to detect movement directly below them? Wouldn't a prudent contractor have set them to act in a vertical plane as well? After all, burglars, unless they couldn't avoid it, shunned open places. They dressed in dark clothes and hugged walls, much as he was doing now!

He decided to contact Aileen right then, before going any further. So if he did trigger the lights Driggs' first impression, once he'd shaken the sleep out his eyes, would be that she was the offender. Bulkily clothed as he was, he rather awkwardly produced his mobile phone from an inner pocket, dialled the first number in the memory and allowed it to ring three times. He was rewarded by the noise of an engine starting carried on the north-east wind as he began to inch along the front of the farmhouse.

Lauder reached the side of the wall of the porch without the lights activating just as Aileen pulled through the entrance to the property. He stood behind the potted evergreen and watched, watched as the carnival came to town!

The oncoming car drove steadily along the drive, its blazing headlights washing one way and then another across the face of the farmhouse. An old but still serviceable ghetto blaster – which Lauder vaguely remembered as belonging to Jim – played Dire Straits' Sultans of Swing at top volume from the back seat, while from the front, at equal volume and provided by the CD deck in the car's sound system Meatloaf belted forth 'Bat out of Hell.' Sound waves were reinforcing one another, gouging and mutilating one another, and the result was a cacophony of noise which had Lauder raising his hands to his ears.

The Vauxhall reached the end of the drive slowed to a stop, and the outside lights snapped on. Now coupled with the car's lights the place was lit up like a football stadium. Aileen stood at the beginning of the turning area – engine revving, lights dazzling, music blaring. It was as if she was saying, "I'm sticking it to you... What are you going to do about it?"

And 'sticking it to them' she was, Lauder realised. Now there were lights on inside the house, and he was sure he'd heard the sound of a raised voice. Aileen must have sensed the message had sunk in too. She put the car in gear, moved onto the tarmac apron and began to turn back onto the drive.

At that moment the door of the house was wrenched open. Lauder from his shadowy vantage saw a burly figure pass the side window of the porch, wrestle for a few seconds with the outside door and then explode into the open. A man who could only be Driggs, red faced and cursing, halted momentarily to look wildly about him. He saw the retreating Vauxhall and, one hand trying to restrain a flapping dressing gown, the other hand cradling a broken shotgun, started to lurch after it. Aileen must have seen Driggs' appearance in the rear mirror because she regained the drive and began to gradually accelerate.

That was Lauder's cue. He smartly ducked from his cover, entered the porch and in three more strides was inside the house. The hall was large, oak-panelled, and empty he saw with a sigh of relief. He thought he heard a noise upstairs but with the racket coming from outside he couldn't be sure.

Suddenly a new sound, penetrating and riding above the others, reached him. It was the high-pitched whine of a protesting engine. Lauder turned from an examination of the small cloakroom beneath the stairs and, not wanting to believe his ears, hurried back to the front door.

It was plain what had happened. A group of ewes had stopped running, and were now looking back with the mixture of stupidity and amazement which only sheeps' expressions can convey. The object of their gaze was the Vauxhall. It was askew and off the drive, its wheels skidding and throwing up mud from the waterlogged ground. Clearly Aileen had been compelled to swerve in order to avoid hitting the sheep. The senseless animals must have bolted in front of her when she was almost abreast of them.

Lauder saw Driggs arrive at the car, hurl open the drivers door and level his shotgun, What happened then was a blank. He was completely unconscious of crossing the intervening distance between them. One moment he was watching Driggs point the gun at Aileen, the next, impelled by a terrible rage, he was crashing into him.

The farmer was knocked off his feet, the gun falling harmlessly beside him. Lauder swooped down on it, and then turning saw from Aileen's weak smile she was unhurt. He looked down at Driggs who, swearing vilely and breathing hard, had hauled himself up onto his knees.

"This," he spat out, "is the only thing guns are good for!" and he hurled the weapon over the car roof to disappear into the night sky.

Driggs watched unbelievingly as his valuable Purdey vanished from sight. It was another outrage heaped on the earlier ones. Fury gripped him again, ushering away the fright from the unexpected attack. "I'll settle your hash," he bellowed, "you woolly-headed bastard!" and rising to his feet he swung his right fist.

Lauder moved inside the clumsy punch, feeling it flick his left ear. Then as he blocked another crude blow he fixed on Driggs' paunch, obligingly on show because of his gaping pyjamas. Old advice from a different time flashed through his mind. "Let the man's momentum bring him onto you, then hit six inches beyond the target," the NCO had drummed into them.

And as if the years had stood still, Lauder drove a vicious jab into the farmer's solar plexus. There was an expulsion of air and Driggs sat down, solidly and suddenly. He sat for five seconds like an effigy of Buddha – stock still, eyes vacant, each leg tucked under the other. Then a flicker of vomit appeared at his lips, followed by a gush and he emptied his stomach. He rolled over sideways, moaning and clutching his abdomen.

Lauder looked at Driggs then at Aileen, still belted into her seat, so rapid had been the violent exchange. "I don't think he'll bother us for a while," he said hoarsely, flexing his gloved hand.

"Yes," was all Aileen could manage to say. She glanced at the prostrate farmer and then back at Lauder. She'd suspected Iain in extenuating circumstances could act as he had. And now it was confirmed, a certain degree of awe was supplementing the other emotions crowding in on her.

A series of shouts and cries travelled across the floodlit expanse between them and the farmhouse. A small fat woman, made even less prepossessing by curlers and a bilious-yellow dressing gown, was wringing her hands with alarm. She saw Lauder looking back, and with a further wail ran into the house.

He turned to Aileen, his expression grim. "Bloody lights," he cursed. "She must have bypassed the time switch. We've got to get out of here!"

"What can we do?" she quailed, her face whitening.

"No cause for panic yet," he said, inwardly collecting himself at the sight of her reaction. "What we do is take the carpet inserts from both wells of the front seats, and tuck them under the front wheels. You're not far from the tarmac so they just need to grip for a second, and we've cracked it."

"Right," Aileen said, clearly relieved at his response. She got out of the car and bent to begin yanking the floor covering from beneath the control pedals.

Lauder momentarily put his hand on her shoulder and then hurried round to the other side to do the same. He felt much more worried than his manner had indicated. Mrs Driggs would have phoned '999' by now, and they had perhaps ten minutes before the police arrived. The offences were mushrooming rapidly – trespass, disturbing the peace and the latest one of assault. He didn't mind so much for himself, it was a risk he was reconciled to. But the thought of Aileen being implicated was too abhorrent to contemplate.

The front wheels were embedded in the soft earth to a depth of about three inches. Lauder pushed the piece of matting as far under the rear of his tyre as he could. He then looked below the chassis of the Vauxhall and saw Aileen had done the same. "They just need to bite once," he called over to her, glancing at the drive a few yards away, "and we'll be all right."

Aileen nodded. "What do you want me to do next?" she asked, brushing the dirt from her hands.

"Get in, start the car and engage reverse when I shout."

As Lauder reached the front of the vehicle, Driggs staggered to his feet three yards from him. The man paid him no attention but began, head slightly bowed, to walk slowly towards the house. Aileen watched him from the driver's seat then looked questioningly at Lauder. He shook his head. He had seen the condition before and knew Driggs was no longer a threat. His NCO had been most eloquent on the subject, "99.9 percent of us can't take punishment," he used to expound. "Boxers can because the silly buggers train themselves to take stick, but the rest of us can't. Deliver a good thump to any of three areas – chin, solar plexus or testicles, and the contest is over. Forget the crap Hollywood serves up; if somebody hits you properly it's fini, goodnight and where's my bed."

And as Driggs shuffled his way to the front door, Lauder was sure the man would give them no more trouble that night. Trouble was coming from another quarter now, and probably at about eighty miles per hour!

With a small invocation he grasped the bumper, shouted to Aileen and pushed with all his strength. The next moment the bonnet in front of him was bucking and twisting like a crazy horse; the blur of two pieces of carpet sailed past him, then suddenly the car was no longer there. Lauder found himself face down on the sodden ground with the certain knowledge that most of his right leg was lying in a large puddle. He raised his head and tried to wipe some of the mud from his eyes. Ahead of him a very dirty Vauxhall purred on the drive.

"Are you all right?" Aileen called anxiously beginning to open the car door.

He hauled himself upright and walked towards her. Better than I was a minute ago," he said, grinning. "Hop in the other side, I'll drive."

Lauder wrenched the ski mask from his head, and without a backwards glance drove as quickly as he could out of the farm property. Two minutes later, the faint yet piercing sound of a siren reached them as they turned off the military road bound for their village.

"Phew," Aileen exclaimed, a slight tremor in her voice, "that was too close a call for comfort."

"Much too close" he murmured.

She suddenly reached out to stroke the hand nearest her on the steering wheel. "I'm really sorry, Iain," she said quietly, "to have got you into this mess."

"Don't talk like that," he said roughly. "You couldn't help it, I would have swerved too. Our luck ran out, that's all – it was just a combination of circumstances, spooked sheep and soaking ground that went against us."

"It's big of you to say so," Aileen said, kneading his hand, "but it's still a mess."

Lauder didn't say anything. As much as he would prefer to think otherwise, he knew Aileen was right. The danger was no longer immediate but it still very much existed. For the unpalatable fact was that the Driggs knew the registration of the Vauxhall. There were only two options open to him as he saw it, both of them far from perfect and only capable of limiting the trouble. The question was which one would limit the damage most?

"Will you report your car stolen then, Iain?" Aileen asked.

Lauder's head swung round to look at her directly. Then he quickly returned his gaze to the road. He supposed he would get used to it eventually. But once more she'd surprised him with the speed and clarity of her mind. She had analysed the debacle back at the farm, identified the consequences arising from it, and by the way her question was phrased – and unlike him – had already decided what the best course of action was.

"I think so," he said. "It seems the best tack in what is basically a no-win situation."

"There's no chance then that they haven't got the registration number?"

"No," Lauder said emphatically. "The Driggs woman alone got a really good look at the car. After all, she was barely twenty yards away and the whole bloody place lit up like a mid-week football match."

"So the police will be able to trace the car back to you."

"They will," Lauder said bitterly. "I could get a visit tomorrow. I wish to hell I'd masked some of the letters on the plates."

Privately, he was cursing himself. It was all so unnecessary, he couldn't help feeling. Had he been strong, stuck to his original convictions and kept Aileen out of it, then they wouldn't be in their present predicament. The Vauxhall wouldn't have been part of the plan if he'd acted alone. He would have looked elsewhere for diversion – kept things much simpler. But now the cat, with a capital C, was about to leap out of the bag. They could end up with both the police and the Hunt on their backs!

"We've got no choice then, have we," Aileen said in a

small voice. "Ditching the car is the only thing we can do. It's either that, or the police will start mounting a case against us."

Lauder nodded. "That's about the size of it. It's the Vauxhall which ties us to the farm. Remove it from the picture and we'll muddy the water for them. Driggs has no idea who I am, and I don't think he got a good look at you, did he?"

"No, he didn't," she replied. "The light was poor inside the car, and with this headscarf and heavy coat I'm wearing he couldn't see much of me anyway." Then as if prompted she pulled the scarf free, shaking and pushing her fair hair into place.

Lauder glanced at her, then turned back to the road. He could now see the three solitary street lights of their village, picking out the blackness of the rising ground in front of them. "So that's it," he said. "I'll drop you off at your place, then I'll dump the car."

"You'd best drop me off at the edge of the village. We don't want some insomniac of a busybody seeing us outside my front door."

"Of course... you're right," Lauder murmured. He shook his head as he left the main road to approach the village. Again Aileen had shown her quality. Perhaps he was tired but she seemed to have an altogether better grasp of the situation than he. The fact was they were existing on borrowed time. There were two thieves supposed to be sitting in their places right now! While he'd seen the necessity to part company with the Vauxhall, Aileen had already worked out the implications arising from it.

Lauder pulled the car next to a hedge and came to a stop. About thirty yards ahead the street lights illuminated the lane running through the hamlet.

"Have you decided where you're going to leave it?" Aileen asked, disengaging her seat belt.

"I thought Hallridge – it seems as good a place as any."

"So I'll wait ten minutes and then come to seek you."

"No, Aileen," he said stretching out for her hand. "Too

much coming and going will only attract attention. I'll make my own way back."

"But, Iain," she cried, "it's ten-past one, and Hallridge is all of six miles away. You won't get back until nearly dawn."

"It's more like four overland. I've walked it before and it's not bad ground.... I reckon on about an hour and a half."

Aileen didn't argue further, but suddenly leaned forward to give a fierce kiss on his mouth. "Ring me as soon as you can," she breathed.

He gave a hollow laugh. "I'll be in touch in the morning, if I can get myself out of bed."

Lauder watched her hurry up the lane to disappear through the third garden gate in a row of terraced houses. He engaged gear, swung the car round and, grim-faced, drove away from the village for the second time that night.

CHAPTER SEVEN

The alarm clock jangled, and Lauder came protestingly out of oblivion. He looked at the offending object and saw it was eight-fifteen. He'd been in bed for all of five hours. He threw the duvet back, swung his legs out of bed and yawningly crossed the room. He drew the curtains and stopped for a moment to look out of the window. It was a morning habit and one he never tired of. For the truth was that the view the window commanded had caused him to buy the house.

Lauder stood, stroking the stubble on his chin, gazing from right to left and back again. His predecessor, the previous owner, had been a wise man. He'd seen the potential of the rather basic, one-bedroomed cottage. All it needed, he must have reasoned, to transform good views into awesome ones, was height. So with one master stroke he'd had a loft conversion done, installing the bathroom the house lacked and a dormer bedroom next to it. And the result was a panorama which made everyone who saw it gasp. Before him, in the brittle sunlight of early morning, stretching from the coastal plain in the east to the smudgy blue of the Pennines in the west, was almost the whole layout of the Tyne's course, a cross section of Northumberland, bordered by the Durham hills to the south, which was about fifty miles long.

Lauder turned away from the scene and went to the bathroom. Normally he savoured the views but that wouldn't be the case today. He had the role of outraged car owner to play, nor was there much time for delay. If the police contacted him first then he would lose a lot of credibility. He must be the one to approach them, be the hapless victim of yet another car crime.

He washed quickly then returned to the bedroom where he picked up the bedside phone. A minute later after dialling '999' he was talking to the desk sergeant at Hexham Police Station. The officer, a man called Greaves, was courteous but noncommittal until Lauder, in response to one of his questions, revealed the registration number of the Vauxhall.

"I see," the sergeant commented. "We think a car of that description and registration was involved in an incident in the early hours of this morning."

"You mean a robbery... something like that?" Lauder said ingenuously.

"No, it wasn't that," the officer replied. "Look, sir... are you going to be at home for the rest of the day?"

"I wasn't planning on going out." Lauder answered.

"Good," the sergeant said. "It's just that one of my colleagues, Sergeant Young, is the investigating officer. He's off duty at the moment, doesn't start again until late afternoon but I'm sure he'll want a word with you."

"Anything that helps find my car," Lauder said forcibly, "and the bugger who took it."

The sergeant assured him if there were any early developments they'd let him know, then rang off. Lauder went downstairs to begin preparing his breakfast. So far, he reflected as he loaded the toaster with bread, his tactics for the police seemed to be panning out quite well. Just as he'd anticipated, the Driggs had been able to supply the Vauxhall's particulars. So his long, stumbling walk last night, plus his recent histrionics as the bereft car owner, had so far averted serious trouble. He was by no means clear or free yet, but he'd established a position which the police would find great difficulty in budging.

On the other hand he knew he was in deep trouble with the Hunt. The Driggs would have received an incident number from the police, and once his car was recovered it would just be a matter of time before they got to know the vehicle belonged to him, and how the two thieves, still at large unfortunately, had stolen the car and then proceeded to be beastly to them. Mrs Driggs and a few more people might accept the story. But he knew the hard-nosed element like Henshaw and Driggs wouldn't. He suspected they'd been waiting for him to make a mistake and now he'd obliged them. They couldn't, of course, be entirely sure at first. They would have to make some enquiries. However once they established he loathed their activities, had a woman friend in the village and was the same height and build as Driggs' assailant, they would be certain.

And what then, Lauder pondered as he sipped coffee and started to spread marmalade on his toast – what would they do? Well, it would be a lot more than an organised flower bed trampling, he was sure of that. They would probably come for him at night just as he'd gone to them. He'd been outside the law, and they would feel justified in acting the same way. But he knew if he confronted the question head on, thought about it as dispassionately as he could, that was where similarities stopped. For when they came they would intend to hurt him. He'd aggravated them too much, too often! The task would be seized on by the nastiest, the wildest within the core of the Hunt. There would be a few wanting to give him a savage beating.

Lauder found himself perspiring. He wiped his brow and took a long drink of coffee to counteract a dry mouth... What could he do? Or more accurately what couldn't he do, and therefore what was left? He knew he couldn't go to the police. Apart from the fact that he hadn't been threatened yet, to approach them would undermine the position he'd just contrived. It would push them into thinking his tale was a hoax, that it was he who had been at the Driggs' farm, after all.

Nor was removing himself an option. He had an old friend in Edinburgh who'd been wanting him to visit for some time. But to leave now would be to go against the grain, and besides, he knew, he'd simply be deferring the evil day.

So there it was – up close and unnerving. It seemed he had little choice other than resisting. The odds would be unequal. But if he prepared carefully, neutralised the advantage of surprise, then he might be able to do just enough to deter them. One thing was for sure though, he thought darkly. This time none of them would get the chance to intimidate Aileen.

*

Ben, tail wagging as usual, lumbered up to the top of the hill. He stopped and looked expectantly back at Aileen. She lengthened her stride, calling to him. The early evening was fine with a moderate wind blowing, and the walk was doing her good. It had helped to digest her tea and what Iain had imparted on the telephone at mid-day while she was at work.

The initial news about the police was encouraging – they seemed to have accepted the scenario of the stolen car. Her mouth tightened – she didn't at all like subterfuge. But in light of the events last night she couldn't see what else they might have done. Iain and she, and for compelling reasons, had simply intended to make nuisances of themselves. The situation wouldn't have escalated into violence but for Driggs pointing a shotgun at her. In which case there was no way they were prepared to face criminal charges brought by a person like him. Someone who thought fun was rending a beautiful animal to pieces most weekends.

It seemed there was a substratum of this type at every level of society. Only yesterday she'd read aghast about four men on Teesside who'd unearthed a badger colony, then stood laughing at their bull-mastiffs butchering the terrified creatures. Anger stained Aileen's already pink cheeks. Driggs and his kind had no innate decency, were callous to the suffering they caused, and she was sure there were more like him at the centre of the Hunt. Which made it doubly disturbing that they must very soon learn Iain's identity!

Yet his attitude on the telephone had been puzzling. She knew that a logical mind would have thought it through – examined the likely repercussions from the foul -up last night. But he'd been surprisingly low key, referring to how he must shortly expect his quota of flower-trampling and insults. She'd questioned his analysis, pointing out that in her view he would soon be a target for the meanest in the Hunt, that he ought to expect some sort of violent reprisal. But again he'd been dismissive, saying he had the idea of visiting Nigel in Edinburgh – a divorcee too and one of his oldest friends – for a few days. So if the wild men were of that mind, they'd have no-one to play with.

The thought of his Scottish excursion irked her. Not in the sense that she resented his going – it wasn't that. Aileen was happy he enjoyed Nigel's friendship and others besides. It was just that she felt she'd missed something. Iain wasn't the sort to defer problems, it was out of kilter with his character. He chose to meet and deal with them as they arose. If an element of the Hunt meant to harm him, they wouldn't be deterred by his absence for a few days. So what was going on?

She climbed a stile and walked up the small road leading into the village. There was no-one around, which was typical. During the brief summer there were always people around – chatting, tending their gardens, walking. But once the cooler weather of autumn arrived most of her neighbours were only to be seen through misted windscreens and at the end of upraised arms. She turned and went through the garden gate, her mind returning to the puzzle.

Aileen knew she was lucky. For the first time in over twenty years she had someone who cared deeply for her. The only daughter of a headmaster and his wife, she'd gone to the altar a loved and protected girl and married a mirror image of herself. Unfortunately, from there, while she'd progressed into womanhood, Robbie had remained a boy. Big, open-faced and charming, he never shook off the notion that the world was ordered solely for him. She was increasingly left to tend to family and home alone, while he, if not pursuing his latest enthusiasm – rally driving, shooting, salmon fishing – was drinking with his rugby friends. Then as the novelty of her also waned, he started philandering. She wasn't aware of it for a long time – she'd taken a lecturing job and Robbie was never around much anyway. Besides, he was careful. Their erratic love life continued, there were no phone calls, no lingering traces of another perfume. But then, perhaps emboldened by the attention cronies were giving his exploits, his discretion began to slip. Until the monumental embarrassment occurred, of mother with teenage son on her arm encountering father with current mistress, in the melee of a theatre cocktail bar.

Iain had shaken his head in disbelief when she first recounted the story. Like many men in the area he'd heard of her ex-husband's promiscuity. He maintained he hadn't realised the man's stupidity until he got to know her; saying – and this invariably made her blush – that Robbie must have been brain-dead to have sought hamburgers outside the home when there was best quality steak in it.

Aileen, as intuitively feminine as any of her gender, knew Iain was very happy with the treatment he was receiving. But he was wrong in assuming Robbie had once got the same. A woman acted as she felt – she couldn't do otherwise; and she was no exception. Unlike Iain he'd never listened to her concerns, rarely made her laugh, seldom took her anywhere….The list was endless and it had the inevitable effect on their love life.

She suddenly stopped in the midst of removing her coat. She stood one arm in, the other out, as the full realisation hit her. Care, the antonym to what had characterised Robbie's behaviour, was the key. It had been the wonderful feature of the last ten months. A stark contrast to the arid years with her ex-husband. With Iain she was the beneficiary of all sorts of considerate acts. She just needed to shiver on the golf course or coming into the open air and he was removing his coat to give her; if a pavement was in disrepair he took her arm; every time he stayed overnight there was a tray of toast, marmalade, coffee and fruit juice brought to her in the morning. And as she opened the kitchen door to let Ben wearily plod towards his basket, she knew that he was watching out for her once more.

His assessment was no different to hers. He was expecting trouble, and meant to keep her out of it. She saw that Iain's surprise decision to journey to Edinburgh was almost certainly a pretence. It was simply a ploy to keep her away. She was usually through those familiar doors twice or thrice a week but in-line with what she suspected, Iain had been quite insistent about visiting her tonight. He intended to temporarily break that pattern – make sure she wasn't around when the wild ones came calling. Knowing by now the sort of man she had, she decided he would already be preparing. He'd be reasoning when the attack would come, what form it would take and how best to deal with it.

Out of the disaster at Driggs' farm he'd seen the opportunity to do them irreparable harm. There would be no shouts for help from Iain, no attempt at conciliation, no bid to escape. Knowing him, he would have reasoned his only chance was a running battle, keeping them at bay until help arrived. And in resisting them he would be banking on the struggle becoming uglier. So when the police did arrive the beasts would be seen for what they really were!

Aileen found herself shaking. She grasped the arm of the nearest chair and sat down heavily. Her mind was screaming. What on earth could Iain do! Resourceful and brave though he was, there were bound to be at least two, possibly three, against him. He couldn't beat such odds, and if things got out of hand there was no telling where it might end!

The panic suddenly fled Aileen's face, replaced by an expression pure with resolve. It was no good having the vapours, she fiercely chided herself. She too could do some contingency planning. And the first thing to establish was, had the nasty element at the heart of the Hunt begun to act yet? Due to the demands of the 'Neighbourhood

Watch' she could recognise what the locals drove, so a strange vehicle moving through or parking up near the village would stand out. That was the tack to take and the sooner she started the better!

*

Lauder looked at the elder of the two policemen sitting next to him. "And you say, sergeant, that the station received news of my car by early afternoon. That's unusual isn't it – for a stolen vehicle to be reported so quickly."

"It is, sir," Young replied, meeting Lauder's gaze and holding it. "Normally a car lies around for a day or so before it's reported. But it seemed the thieves abandoned your Vauxhall right in front of Miss Terry's window. She's a spinster and loves the views her cottage has. The villagers know better than to obstruct it; so when she discovered neither of the neighbours had visitors she became suspicious and phoned us."

The young constable farthest away from Lauder, glanced up from his notebook. "She's a very public-spirited lady," he ventured, "she's got…" He tailed off, seeing the sergeant's expression.

"Are you getting all the main points down, Gore?" the sergeant said pointedly.

The earnest face stiffened, he swallowed and his eyes dropped to the notebook once more.

Young moved his considerable frame into another position in the armchair. The gas fire, around which the three chairs made a semi-circle, was warm, and the colour of his crab-apple complexion was beginning to heighten. "It seems odd to me, sir," he said, "that your car was taken from here, appeared at the Driggs' farm and then was dumped at Hallridge, the next village to this."

Lauder was unperturbed. "The next village, as you put it, is six miles away. Besides whoever took my car – I believe you said there were two of them – would have to park their car somewhere."

"But why park up there?" Young persisted. "It's north of here. They went to the Driggs' farm after lifting your vehicle, so why didn't they park their car somewhere between the two places?"

Lauder realised it was time to show his temper. "How would I know, sergeant?" he said with asperity. "Surely it's your job to catch these people, and then you can ask them. Perhaps the thieves didn't park their car at Hallridge. Perhaps they simply made the switch there – one dumping my car and the other driving him off. Perhaps they didn't have a car... The permutations seem endless....I really don't know!"

If Young was ruffled by Lauder's tone he didn't reveal it. He glanced unconcernedly at Gore scribbling furiously and back at him. "What puzzles me, sir," he said, "at first sight they seem like joy-riders and then the similarities stop. One made a detour on foot, and from the descriptions we've got they certainly weren't kids."

Lauder scrutinised the man for a moment. He knew he mustn't be drawn, that he'd already been on the verge of saying too much. "It does seem curious, sergeant," he said, then parrying the statement, "but I have neither your experience nor training to make a judgement in these matters."

Young regarded Lauder impassively for a moment. "You did say, didn't you, sir," he said questioningly, "that you didn't go out last night?"

"I did," Lauder said levelly.

"Did you hear any noises then – voices, tools being used,...your own engine kicking into life?"

"No, I didn't."

"That seems a bit odd to me sir, a car lifted from an isolated spot like this, right under your nose. And you didn't hear anything. I thought you country people could pick up on anything out of the ordinary."

"This country person went to bed about eleven-thirty last night, sergeant." Lauder replied. "The walls are thick, the bedroom's at the other side of the house and as I recall

I slept soundly."

Young grunted and eased himself into another position in the armchair. Lauder watched him, wondering where he would begin probing next.

"And you don't much care for hunting with dogs, do you sir?" the policeman said, "particularly when it's rumoured they sometimes run down a fox."

"No I don't, along with several million others." Lauder replied waspishly, while choking off the response that it was against the law and the police should do more to enforce it. "But I don't exactly see what you're driving at, sergeant. All I know is my car has been stolen and I believe I have the right to enquire if you're making any progress in finding the people who took it!"

"Nobody at Hallridge saw anything," Young said, standing up. "But we're working on it, aren't we Gore!"

The young man stopped writing and reached for his helmet. "Yes, sergeant, we are." he replied, hurriedly getting to his feet.

Lauder accompanied them to the door. The sergeant stopped there and raised his arm to clasp the post, his frame blocking out much of the light from the outside lamp. "So you'll come to the station tomorrow to deal with the formalities, and pick up your car," he said. "You'd better bring your papers too; we'll want to see those before we release it,"

Yes, Lauder thought, and woe betide me if any of the documents are out of order. "Is the car all right then?" he asked.

"The officer who brought it in said there were no problems," Young chuckled. "It needs a damned good wash though."

Lauder nodded. "Incidentally, sergeant," he said, "how did you know I was against the Hunt?"

The shrewd blue eyes studied Lauder once again. "I didn't," he replied. "But Mr Driggs rides with the Hunt, and since somebody assaulted him last night I'm inclined to think it's more to do with that than joy-riders."

Young stood, a big authoritative man, smiling slightly, completely sure of himself, gazing at Lauder with the inexperienced constable hovering behind him. "Well," he said finally, "we must be off. Take good care, won't you, sir."

Lauder raised a hand as the police car gradually accelerated up the drive. You big, bright bastard, he thought, turning away with a small but rueful smile playing about his mouth. The man had already worked out what had happened. He would have enormous difficulty in proving it, of course. But Lauder knew he would have to be doubly careful in the coming days, and that his copy book was irretrievably blotted for the future. The police didn't like 'clever buggers' as a friendly acquaintance – now a detective inspector in Liverpool – had once described them. Offenders rather than criminals, who after breaking the law then set about putting themselves beyond it. They went onto an unofficial black list, he claimed, which most stations ran, and this effectively disqualified them from any leniency from the police, no matter how minor the offence. Nowadays people generally presented themselves to the world from within their cars. So Lauder knew in future if a tail light wasn't functioning, if he drove at thirty-two miles an hour, he was for it when the police were around. The word on him would be going out!

But aside from that he had to hand it to Young – the man had been impressive, very impressive. He'd probably manoeuvred Driggs into admitting he'd thrust a shotgun into the woman's face, and therefore understood how the beating had come about; he'd realised the significance of the walkabout, and grasped it was some sort of protest that had gone wrong. Certainly, with him, Lauder reflected, the sergeant had seemed in control, one step ahead of him right throughout the interview. Young must have not only arrived at what happened, but also worked out how he would react to his questioning. He pulled a wry face when he thought of how the sergeant had led him into discussing the motives and actions of the fictional thieves. An innocent man wouldn't have been drawn in that way. He now saw the attitude he'd adopted must have confirmed his guilt in Young's eyes. It was difficult to accept but the fact remained that he, who'd first thought himself the intellectual superior of the sergeant, had been thoroughly out-thought by the man. He remembered the policeman he'd once known saying that after a time a good copper could tell if someone was guilty; the big problem often was, the man had conceded, producing the evidence to prove it in a court of law.

And that was precisely Young's quandary. While the man had outsmarted him in the interview he still had no proof to connect him with the fiasco at the Driggs' farm. He could try Aileen, of course. Lauder had thought it best to mention her when asked about a woman friend, reasoning Young would find out anyhow, and secondly – now completely risible in retrospect – that to appear frank and cooperative would help allay suspicion. But somehow he didn't think the sergeant would pursue that line. He was the man's main target. Young would have realised that Aileen's role was only peripheral, and that undoubtedly by now she'd been primed to adopt the 'eyes fluttering…early to bed' routine should he make a call.

Lauder returned to the lounge, sat down and stretched his legs out to the fire. The big question now remaining, he mused, was what would the redoubtable sergeant do next? There was a 'clever bugger' around, someone who was guilty of trespass, assault, disturbing the peace, and, in the matter of the stolen car, conspiring to pervert the course of justice. He wouldn't like that at all. The crime figures had gone up on his patch, and at the same time two fingers had been metaphorically raised in his face.

Lauder had placed Young as one of the old school. The sort of policeman who twenty five years ago – in a much less politically-correct age – would sometimes mete out justice himself; the kid caught shop lifting subjected to a terrible tongue lashing, the local bully given a hiding behind the town's fish and chip shop….that kind of thing.

And with the lawful process apparently now bogged down, he wouldn't be surprised if that experience, those leanings, were stirring. Young might well be on the brink of nudging the course of natural justice!

He could imagine the scenario. The Driggs would be expecting a progress report, and perhaps tomorrow night, when it was even more evident the situation had hardened, Young would call on them. There'd be some pointed inferences made. Lauder could see the car thieves portrayed as having vanished without a trace – no fingerprints, no evidence of a switch car... almost as if they'd never existed! But one good thing – Mr Lauder, the owner had got his car back, undamaged, quite quickly. "Did they know him?" "No, .. nice fellow, ex-army, has a woman friend living in the same village."

Lauder could imagine another scenario too, except this time he saw it from Young's standpoint. The scene Hexham high street perhaps in a week's time; he walking with a pronounced limp or sporting a black eye, or both, the squad car slowing to a halt beside him for Young to emerge and enquire solicitously about his condition, then the ill-concealed satisfaction, the smiles behind hands as the vehicle drew away. That or something similar would suit the sergeant...the 'clever bugger' overtaken by rough justice, in receipt of much deserved retribution.

Lauder scowled. Where his and Young's scenarios differed was that if he wasn't very careful he wouldn't be able to walk down any high streets in a week's time. The sergeant had only seen the tip of the iceberg, had no idea of the reservoir of hate which had accumulated. He wasn't going to be brought to account for one night, but for a whole season of harassment. He shivered and stretched his hands out to the fire.

*

Clive Henshaw drove fast through the night, the large Volvo's headlights illuminating the blackness ahead. He'd taken the phone call from the Driggs about twenty minutes ago and had immediately set off for his farm.

Two thoughts kept recurring, had occupied him since he left the outskirts of Hexham ten minutes earlier. The first was the elation of knowing he could well be on the verge of identifying the twat who'd been plaguing them for the last year or so. He hardly dare build on the brief account Driggs had given him, it seemed too good to be true. Not only had the turd made the mistake he'd prayed for but it had been a colossal one. So much so he'd been forced to come up with some half-cocked story about a stolen car in a bid to get the police off his back.

The smile subsided on his fleshy face as the second thought occurred again. He would have to make it plain to Driggs that he was handling the situation from now on. He knew the man had little time for him, was fond of challenging his authority in that cutting, superior way he had. So he would have to spell it out that it was a Hunt issue and, as Master, he was taking control.

Henshaw scowled. More often than not he had to fight to assert himself. It wasn't just in Hunt matters either... business, social relations, were rarely easy. He sometimes thought because he'd inherited the farm and the shops from his father, people were disinclined to treat him with the respect he was due. Moreover, as Elaine hadn't managed to give him any children – though, of course, he never mentioned her infertility – he felt it exaggerated their attitude towards him. So you had to stamp your presence on people and situations – let them know they'd best tread carefully on anything which concerned you, that you wouldn't tolerate any shit from anyone.

He reached the stone pillars marking the entrance to the farm, turned right and glided the quarter of a mile along the tarmac drive. The outside lights snapped on as the car slowed to a stop in front of the house. Henshaw got out and made a dash for the door, pulling his collar up against the chilly wind as he did so. He rang the bell and within thirty seconds Driggs appeared on the threshold.

"Come inside, Clive," he said brusquely. "Here, let me take your coat."

Henshaw handed over the garment. "Thanks, Archie," he replied, "it's certainly a cold one tonight." He started towards the half open door which Driggs had indicated.

"Where's Vera?" he enquired as his host followed him into the room.

"She's in bed," Driggs said dryly. "She's still upset by the other night, and it's twenty past ten."

If there was an implied criticism Henshaw chose to ignore it. "First time I've been in your inner sanctum, Archie," he remarked, his eyes roving the study. "I've got to say you do yourself proud."

Two walls of the room from floor to ceiling featured row after row of leather-bound books. There was a large, oil-painted landscape occupying sole position on the wall where the door was, which even to Henshaw's untutored eye projected a mastery of light and form. The remaining wall was covered with velvet burgundy coloured drapes and provided a backdrop to a huge, expensive-looking desk. Two leather armchairs grouped round a gas fire completed the furnishings, and it was to one of these that Driggs, now with a slightly amused look on his face, waved him.

"You'll have your usual to drink I take it, Clive?"

"That will be fine, Archie," Henshaw said. He watched Driggs busying himself at the small table next to the desk. The man, he noticed, was carrying himself rather stiffly. Some of his movements particularly when bending forward looked decidedly uncomfortable.

He took the glass of whisky from Driggs and nodded his appreciation. "You mentioned the bastard had whacked you," he commented, as the farmer carefully lowered himself into the other armchair.

"That's right, I'm still sore," Driggs said ruefully. "We were woken up by what seemed the opening of a fairground outside. But by the time I got downstairs the car was driving away. It swerved though to avoid some sheep, got onto soft ground and was soon stuck. I was bloody fuming... it had all the hallmark of stupid kids acting the goat... so I thought... right, I'll teach the buggers a much needed lesson."

"And what does this Lauder look like?" Henshaw said eagerly.

"Oh, he wasn't in the car – he must have been hidden close to the house. The driver was a woman, probably his. She was well and truly stuck – the wheels were flying around and the car was burying itself. So I wrenched open the door and told her to get out."

"What was she like then?" Henshaw demanded.

"I can't say – I wouldn't recognise her if I saw her on the street tomorrow," Driggs said flatly. "The outside lights were on but she was shadowed by the car. I only saw her for about thirty seconds, and besides she was wearing a headscarf and a thick coat."

"Then what happened?"

"Well, as I said, I was ordering her to get out of the car. The next I know the Purdey's knocked out of my hand and I'm sent flying."

"So the cowardly bastard attacked you from behind!" Henshaw asserted.

Driggs regarded Henshaw for a moment. "He didn't get the better of me like that," he said, "if that's what you're implying."

"What do you mean?"

Driggs looked at Henshaw even longer this time. "I'm not easily rattled," he eventually said, "but I admit I was the other night. First looking up to see this bloody, terrorist-type figure, framed by the lights, above me - black balaclava, dark jerkin - in the process of throwing my gun away. Then secondly, when I went for the swine he put me down almost straight away."

He shook his head. "I've always thought myself fairly hard, but it wasn't a contest."

"He took you by surprise, that's all." Henshaw cried, his voice harsh with anger.

He swallowed some whisky and shot a glance at

Driggs. "What beats me," he said, "is where he came from and what he was up to?"

"The bastard was in the house," Driggs said icily.

"He was what?" Henshaw exploded.

"There were a couple of muddy footprints near the cloakroom. We always leave out farm boots in the porch so it couldn't have been one of us. That's why Vera's so upset."

"I'm not surprised," Henshaw replied, looking grimly at Driggs. "By God, this is a new twist. So he was going to plant those bloody notices all over the house and then let himself out."

"Presumably," Driggs said. "He wouldn't need to do anymore. That sort of thing is calculated to send the ladies climbing up the wall anyway."

"Tell me about it," Henshaw said vehemently. "Dodds' wife, aided and abetted by her idiot GP, is popping vallium like there's no tomorrow."

Driggs looked enquiringly at Henshaw. "Do you know the pig then, Clive...this Lauder?"

"Never heard of him," Henshaw rasped. "But I intend to make the cunt's acquaintance, and very soon...There's no doubt it is him, is there?"

"Not really – he's Mr bloody X all right. Vera got the number and the police have confirmed it's his car. Young, the sergeant in charge, called early this evening and said they'd found neither hide nor hair of any joy-riders...it was as if they'd been 'beamed up', was the expression he used. The implication being, of course, that Lauder cooked up the line of a stolen car to cover his tracks."

"I know that Young – he's no fool."

"Anyway," Driggs said, "any lingering doubts I might have had disappeared when Cecil Smith phoned me about nine."

"Ah,...Cec," Henshaw murmured smiling. He had a soft spot for the farmer who had land in the Rede valley, north of the Tyne. Smith hated spoilers with an intensity which approached fanaticism, and was one of his most consistent supporters.

"I don't know how he'd heard so quickly," Driggs went on. "But when I gave him the background he remembered Lauder. He said there'd been a clash at a mid-week meet some years ago, I think it was before your time as Master. Anyway, Lauder had got out of his car and given them a load of invective. Cecil said he was so insulting he came within a whisker of lashing him across the face, and afterwards he made a point of finding out who he was."

"That puts the lid on it," Henshaw said emphatically. "And another thing's certain, Archie."

"What's that?"

"You can't afford to be involved when Lauder gets his just desserts," Henshaw said conspiratorially. "When the bugger gets the mother and father of a hiding, you've got to be watching Coronation Street with your aunt Matilda."

"I don't watch Coronation Street and I haven't got an aunt of that name," Driggs said pointedly. "But I do accept the advice."

"You do," was all Henshaw could rather lamely say. Driggs' reaction had wrong-footed him; mentally he was prepared for a long, perhaps heated argument. And there was the landowner agreeing with him immediately – he hadn't even needed to shout.

Driggs glanced meaningfully at him "I'm not stupid, Clive," he said. "Why should I, the one who would be suspected first, court trouble when you're more than wiling to settle all scores for the Hunt?"

"You're a cool one, Archie," Henshaw observed. "But you're right – leave me to take care of things."

Driggs partially suppressed a yawn and then smiled. "I'm sure you'll do a splendid job, Clive," he said. "I wouldn't like to be in Lauder's shoes at all."

Henshaw grunted, swallowed the last of his whisky and stood up. He'd got what he wanted and would have left shortly anyway. Driggs' launch into vaudeville - the yawning and the indulgent smile - were unnecessary. He'd forgotten about Driggs' normal attitude towards him in the last half hour, but now there were signs of it returning.

He paused in the hall while shrugging on his coat to glance up the stairs. "Give my regards to Vera, Archie, won't you."

"I will, Clive," Driggs said, ushering him to the door, "and thanks for coming."

Yes, thought Henshaw, walking to the Volvo; he would bet, upset or not, Vera didn't get the idea for an early night until she heard he was coming. If ever there was a cold, distant bitch it was Driggs' wife. He'd known her for years, they moved in the same social circles. But he yet had to see her smile or begin a conversation with him. Hunched against the wind, he reached the car and got in. At least, though, he reflected, Vera's behaviour had been predictable, which was more than could be said of her husband's.

He'd heard of Driggs' charm offensives, the rare occasions when the man would abandon his normal confrontational style and become, by all accounts, surprisingly pleasing. Farm inspectors, revenue officials, anyone with the power to make a difference to him, and, it was said, out trotted a smiling, genial Driggs. Henshaw had experienced a sample of that behaviour tonight, and moreover from a person who'd never made a secret of his dislike for him in the past.

So what was going on? Driggs by nature was far from polite. And police or no police he wasn't the sort to sit on the sidelines when there was a personal score to settle – slap Archie once and he'd slap you back twice as hard. Henshaw grimaced; he couldn't weigh up what was happening. It seemed the landowner had a separate agenda, and for the life of him he was unable to see what it was...

The furrows on Henshaw's brow suddenly disappeared, the jowled face relaxed. It was strange, he conceded, but what was the point of him gnawing over it? He'd got what he wanted! He began to hum to the music playing on the radio as the car descended towards the lights in the Tyne valley.

CHAPTER EIGHT

Lauder saw a medium-sized man approaching him along the aisle. He was wearing a dark green anorak zipped up to the throat, a checked flat cap and an angry expression. A fat, little woman with a worried face trailed a few paces behind him. The man stopped at Lauder's trolley, grasped it by two of its front bars and then spat over the contents.

Spittle trickled down over the two bottles of milk, the lettuce and the loaf Lauder had so far collected. He looked back up to the man, saw the blunt ruddy face, the wide arc of the thin-lipped scowl, the hot eyes.

"I think you've been badly brought up," he said.

A family had witnessed the incident with some disbelief, and the father, thinking violence could be in the offing, was now shepherding his wife and three children away.

"If I was a bit younger," the man ranted. "I'd take you outside and beat the living shit out of you."

"I would say you're at least five years younger than me," Lauder replied, "and now I'm providing you with the motivation." He picked up the loaf, the milk and the lettuce and with arms full, advanced on the man.

The little woman had been pulling on her husband's coat throughout the exchange. "Come away, Wilf, come away," she was repeating with increasing anxiety, and now with Lauder almost up to him the man for the first time responded to his wife's tugging.

"Yours I think," Lauder said unceremoniously, dumping the food into their trolley. "You soiled them, so you eat them."

The man started to frame a filthy expression, but Lauder pushed his face close.

"Don't," he said. "You understand, don't!! The belligerent look on the man's face disappeared, and he nodded.

"I'm going to the toilet now to wash off the filth you've

put on me," Lauder said quietly, "and when I come back you're one Hunt supporter who's not going to give me any trouble, are you?"

The farmer again nodded dumbly as a smartly-dressed man came skidding round the end of the aisle and hurried towards them. News travels fast, Lauder thought, and bad news travels even faster. He remembered the civilised face of the young father shopping close to him, and realised that was the connection.

The store official ignored the farmer and pointedly addressed him. "Is there any trouble, sir? Anything I can help you with?"

"No, nothing at all," Lauder replied. "But thanks very much for asking." He looked bleakly at the farmer once more and then walked away pushing his trolley.

*

Clump, clump....thud, thud... James Davidson strode on with the footfalls of others and his own filling his ears. The Friday evening British Airways flight from Gatwick had just disgorged, and now he along with something like a hundred fellow passengers – the jet had been almost full – were making a determined march down one of the long, carpeted corridors of Newcastle Airport.

He hoped Newcastle wasn't going the way of the London airports. Gatwick, for example, was now so big that, depending on which terminal you were destined for, the aeroplane sometimes had to taxi a couple of miles before the passengers could disembark. He didn't want that for his local airport; with its white-marbled concourse, its large windows, the gay colours of shops and cafeterias, it still gave the impression of a bright and friendly place. But as he passed a boarded-off area and a sign announcing an extension of the main building he wondered how long it would be before the planners had contrived a complete character bypass for the airport.

Davidson emerged from the main building by a set of

swing doors and was gratified to see the courtesy van parked at the far side of the pick-up area. The vehicle belonged to a company whom he used during the autumn and winter months. Situated a couple of miles away, they had covered parking whereas the airport had none; and besides the worry of an engine not starting because of damp, it also saved him tramping across a featureless prairie of tarmac in the dark.

Five minutes later he was pointing his freshly-valeted Land Rover west and towards Hexham. Completely alone now for the first time that day, the thoughts which Davidson had pushed to the back of his mind began to surface. He'd had a rough week. It seemed now his comments to a leading Westminster journalist had been ill-timed. They'd been prompted by the recent announcement from the Cabinet office that a private member's bill to repeal the hunting ban would be introduced in the coming year. He'd told the reporter that he was instrumental to the decision, admitting he'd regularly put pressure on the hierarchy since the Conservatives came to power. His disclosure had made the headlines with him cast as the likely proposer of the new legislation. And now in the press, on television, northern Labour MPs were queuing up to take a swipe at him. One in particular had scathingly remarked that he couldn't recall him making the news over Syria, the mess in the euro zone, the job losses in the public sector. But when it came to renewing a charter to terrorise and kill dumb animals, there he was championing the cause of bestiality.

And if that wasn't bad enough, there was more serious trouble brewing. As headlights streamed towards him in a never-ending succession, he remembered Ralph's tone in their long telephone conversation last night. It appeared the phantom raider had been unmasked. A man called Lauder who'd pushed his luck too far while making a nuisance of himself at the Driggs' farm, which was fine in that now his identity was known the man was emasculated – there'd be no more of the harassment which he seemed to specialise in.

But according to his agent, and where the good news changed to awful, a few of the Hunt were thirsting for the chap's blood. Not for them a dressing down for Lauder and an engineered ride through his vegetable patch, they were intent on physical revenge. Davidson groaned audibly. He'd known Ralph Westwood for over ten years and knew he was neither an alarmist nor given to exaggeration. So when he said he suspected Clive Henshaw was forming a hit squad, there was a serious problem in the making.

Vigilante action normally got out of hand, that was why it was unlawful. But at the behest of someone like Henshaw it was a recipe for disaster. Davidson had observed the Hunt Master at close quarters for several years now, and the man was, in his opinion, as unsavoury as they came. His was a case of arrested development if ever he saw one. They said his old man had been a domineering bastard, and the young Clive increasingly the butt after his entry to the family business at the age of sixteen. Well, like father, like son: Henshaw's standard reaction to problems was aggression, a willingness, often blatant, to squash and trample over anyone who got in his way.

Ralph had said if there was anyone who could deflect Henshaw it was he, that the man respected him and would weigh whatever advice he gave. But Davidson didn't at all share Ralph's belief. He thought it altogether more likely that Henshaw would ignore what he said. This was the man who was the protector, the engine, the leader of the Hunt all rolled into one, and the truth was Lauder had struck repeatedly at his beloved charge over the last year. Whether Lauder knew it or not, his clandestine activities had begun to take a sizeable toll.

He'd badly upset even the stalwarts with all the consequent effect on subscriptions. Henshaw must have thought himself being strangled, the very oxygen of his life gradually being turned off. Lauder had probably caused him more distress than anyone since his father, and for that it seemed the man must pay and violently, unless he could find some way to channel Henshaw's wrath.

A couple of thoughts began to tumble around in Davidson's mind. He frowned – strictly speaking it was nowhere in an MP's remit to think as he was doing. But Henshaw wasn't going to be swayed by anything which observed the niceties of the law. The trick was to come up with a scheme which would drastically discomfort Lauder, and yet keep him out of a hospital bed. Accordingly he could suggest – jokingly, of course – the next meet be staged near the man's home and during the course of the day some of the riders give his lawns a thorough churning. Or the fellow from Ponteland be let loose with his muck sprayer, the one who, so disenchanted with his overdraft arrangements, saw fit to bombard his bank a couple of years ago. It would give Lauder a week of the filthiest sort of cleaning... But even as he formulated the thoughts he realised he was wasting his time.

Davidson might stand up in the House, as he had done for two decades, and skilfully contend that hunting was economically necessary for the countryside, that it represented the best way of culling a pest, that evidence existed which indicated the fox actually enjoyed the chase. It went down well with the landed in the county and much of the rank and file of his own party. But having seen the reality first hand he knew the arguments were fallacies. The fox was often run to exhaustion, the terrified animal sometimes pursued for over an hour before meeting its bloody end. And as to hunting being the most efficient means of culling, it was ridiculous. A shotgun or better still a rifle in the hands of a man with experience and a steady aim could despatch an animal humanely within seconds. No, peel away the spurious layers of the issue and the truth was glaring. Hunting with dogs was just a licence for the worst aspects of human nature to reveal their ugly presence.

There was a black beast within everyone. Davidson

knew. Some were hardly aware of it; the great majority, himself included, had to struggle to keep the beast down. Then there were a few who, despite having the biggest beast, seldom contained it. They enjoyed the feeling of power and liberation the beast's escape gave them – so all too often it ran amok. Every Hunt had a small few of that ilk, and none, he suspected, more typical than Henshaw.

Davidson saw the big sign for the Corbridge intersection looming up in front of him. It pointed to Otterburn and the North via the A68, and was the road home, and it also pointed straight ahead to the West, Carlisle and Hexham. He glanced at his watch – the faithful would be gathering in the constitutional club beneath the photograph of Mrs Thatcher in her blue dress. He hesitated a moment, then turned onto the slip road.

Henshaw placed the foaming drinks on the table and glanced at Kerr and Golightly. It was mid-evening in the snug of the Turk's Head. The room was quiet compared to the din in the bar a few yards away. Two old men, the only other occupants, sat talking in low tones in the far corner. They somehow seemed to fit in with the dark-stained wood and the muted colours of the furnishings which characterised the room.

"I had a look around near Lauder's place this morning," Henshaw said. "I didn't get too close, obviously, but I took some glasses and got a good idea of the layout."

He had a long drink from the pint glass and then reached inside his checked jacket producing a pen and a used envelope. "The cunt's on the far side of the village, away from the other houses, so it makes it easier for us." He began drawing in strong strokes, labelling the main features and talking as he worked.

"The village is on a loop which comes back to the main road," he said as Kerr and Golightly craned forward to see the plan. "It's on the south side of the loop, and Lauder's place is on its own, about quarter of a mile away, at the north end."

Kerr craned forward in his seat even more. "What's that you've inked in next to the house?" he said, pointing at the sketch.

Henshaw broke off to put his pen down. He looked at the terrier man, a wide grin flicking across his face. "You're loving this, aren't you... you bugger!" he cried. "It's right up your street."

Kerr matched the grin. There was an air of barely concealed excitement about him which the alcohol was beginning to loosen. "I don't know what you mean, boss," he said, his grin intensifying into a leer.

"There's a Prudhoe lad in hospital, that's what," Henshaw replied, his expression amused, "with a broken jaw and ribs. And I've heard you two weren't a million miles away last weekend, when it happened."

"That wasn't down to me." Golightly said indignantly, glaring at Kerr.

"That's probably because he got to him first," Henshaw said sarcastically. "Anyway if the pair of you were angels I wouldn't be sat talking to you now."

He studied the drawing for a few seconds and then looked at Kerr. "That's a stand of trees you asked about. It's on the north side of the cottage and only about thirty yards away, so we'll use that as cover to come up to the place."

Golightly took a long swallow of beer, glanced at the sketch and then back at Henshaw. "It makes sense – I've been in that area a few times with the hounds and it's open ground on the other three sides. There's just a quarter moon tonight, but even so why not use the cover if it's there."

"Besides," he added, wiping a hand across his mouth, "the wind's coming from the south so there's less chance of sound carrying."

Henshaw gazed at the whipper-in, not for the first time impressed by the man's practicality, Golightly, just as hard as Kerr, but unlike his friend was possessed of a few brains. He nodded appreciatively. "I hadn't thought of that, but you're right."

"Happen we should cut the phone wire," Kerr interjected, "then if he does hear us he's buggered."

Henshaw swung round to stare at the terrier man as Golightly, his mouth pursing, looked away.

"Listen to '007' and the 'Brain of Britain'," he jeered.

"I just…" Kerr began hotly.

"He'll have a mobile, you dummy," Henshaw sneered, interrupting him. "Living alone and not short of a bob or two, he's bound to be kitted out. Here," he said roughly, reaching inside his jacket to produce a wallet and then a ten pound note, "be useful for once in your life and get the drinks."

Golightly pointed to the envelope as Kerr, scowlingly, left them. "I see the garage is on the other side of the drive," he said "so we best come up in line with it for the last bit."

Henshaw nodded. "You've got the idea."

"And then what?"

"There's a window at the bottom side of the house, hidden from the lane and next to the open fields. I think it belongs to a bedroom. It's a standard window – two sections both opening outwards, and it doesn't seem double-glazed so we should be able to force it without being seen."

Henshaw looked up to see Kerr standing next to him. The man held three pints clasped together in his outstretched hands, and from the reckless grin playing about his face all the ebullience of a few minutes ago had been restored.

"And then when we're in, we'll do the bugger!" Kerr almost bayed, putting the drinks down on the table.

Henshaw saw the two old men in the corner break off their conversation and glance over towards them. He grasped the elasticated band at the bottom of Kerr's bomber jacket and yanked on it. "Sit down, Fred," he snarled, "and bloody shut up."

Kerr guffawed as his bottom slapped the chair. "What

did I do?" he appealed to a silent Golightly. "What did I do?"

Henshaw looked furiously at Kerr and shook his head. He saw the man was still oblivious to the interest he'd caused at the other end of the room, and judging from his present mood he wouldn't much care.

He pulled his chair closer to Kerr's. "Put a bloody lid on it, Fred," he rasped, "or you'll blow the whole thing. Do you want that, you daft sod... Well, do you?"

Golightly saw Kerr's face clouding with resentment. He knew his mate rated Henshaw, saw him as a kindred spirit and the only authority figure he could talk to. But there was a limit even for Henshaw, and he'd just got dangerously close to it.

"Anyway," he said quickly, "when we get inside what are you planning for Lauder?"

Henshaw turned to him, his teeth suddenly baring to reveal a wolfish grin. "I want the bastard to have a memento of the night," he said. "Something, which at his age will give him hockey for the rest of his natural."

He paused, obviously relishing the thought. "So besides the usual cuts, bruises and gore we give him the Tynedale 'pull and stomp'."

Golightly didn't reply, he was too taken aback to do so. He turned to see the mad grin on Kerr's face, and then looked at Henshaw again as the man drained the last of his pint. He'd head-butted a few saboteurs in his time. Been in several fights where bad injuries had happened. He still ruefully remembered being at the receiving end himself when his right arm had been fractured in a drunken brawl. But this would be a first – setting out to cold-bloodedly maim somebody. The Tynedale 'pull and stomp', as Henshaw put it, was an old rugby expression for the breaking of a leg. He shook his head and raised the glass to his lips.

Henshaw rose to his feet, eyeing them. "I have to go to the club, he said. "I'll meet you at midnight in the market square, and in the meantime ease up on the sauce, will you." He looked pointedly at Kerr.

The terrier man returned his gaze. "Is there anything you want us to bring?" he asked.

Henshaw shrugged into a navy blue anorak. "No. I'll bring tools, flashlight…" he stopped momentarily, an unpleasant smile covering his face. "In short, everything we need."

Kerr watched as the burly figure let himself out the side door of the snug. He slowly shook his head and looked at Golightly. "Fucking Conservatives…" he sneered.

*

The television picture switched from the agonised expression of the grey-suited politician back to the interviewer. With a half smile at the corners of his mouth – it had been another satisfactory mauling – Jeremy Paxman began to run through the headlines for the following day's papers. Lauder pressed the stop button on the remote control and glanced at his watch.

It was eleven-fifteen, and if his visitors were coming he reckoned he had about another hour to wait. The indicators were strong. The behaviour of the cretin in the supermarket this morning, the fact that it was now four nights since the debacle at Driggs' farm, and probably the most potent, hot-heads couldn't be diverted for any length of time.

He finished his whisky, stood up and walked into the kitchen. From the window he could see the black outline of the small wood beyond the garage. That was the way they would come, he knew. It would be his choice if he were in their position. There were open fields on all the other three sides of the house. Whereas the approach from the north first provided the wood for cover, and then on the closing stage his garage.

Lauder realised anything he could do in advance to reduce the unequal odds was vital. A crucial factor would be to deny them the advantage of surprise. If he could know to the second when they began making incursions on his property, then help in the form of the police would be that much faster to his door. So he'd been busy that afternoon. The huge gales of a month ago had taken their toll in the wood, and within half an hour of him crossing the field and entering the trees he had what he wanted.

The dry branches, small but thick enough to make a resounding crack when stepped on, he'd spread at two spots along the boundary wall. Slightly raised by flat stones, these were at each of the back corners of the garage. They were the likely spots for anyone using the building as a cover to scale the wall, and to assist them further in their choice he'd dislodged a number of the uppermost stones.

If his early warning system was simple, the means he'd chosen to defend himself was simpler. He'd also cut two good staffs while in the wood that afternoon. About three feet long and over an inch in diameter, one of them now stood propped up against the kitchen table. The other was on the edge of the trees where he could quickly locate it should the need arise. For Lauder was determined that as soon as the nastiness started it would be a running fight. He suspected if cornered he'd be thrashed mercilessly. So it would be hit and run for him, picking off the individual who was too eager or just plain careless. The action, as he hoped to influence it, would begin in the house and then spread to the gardens and the wood. That way, defending himself, retaliating when he could, he intended to use his local knowledge to prolong the struggle until help arrived.

The problem was police reaction times to his locality were generally of the order of thirty-five minutes. It was a very long time to stay unscathed, run the gauntlet of the fists and baseball bats. He hoped for thirty minutes, reasoning a '999' call after twelve wouldn't encounter the normal competition for police resources. But it was somewhat daunting to think his well-being might hang on how rowdy the scene was outside Hexham's night club or whether the town's burglars were out in force.

Lauder returned to the lounge and stood warming himself in front of the fire. Someone who wouldn't be appearing tonight or in the next few days was Aileen, he thought, his face darkening. He'd been awful last night at her place. She'd pressed him about his fictional visit to Edinburgh and got uncomfortably close to the truth. But instead of diverting her in some way, he'd been aggressive – pointing out rather fiercely that, "he didn't need to account to anybody and he'd do damn well as he saw fit." He could still picture the hurt look on her face as he strode from the house with a perfunctory 'goodnight'.

He snorted, his anger with himself unabated. In the business unfolding he knew there was no place for a woman, particularly his woman. But he should have acted differently – she was, after all, only governed by concerns for his welfare...

CHAPTER NINE

It wasn't the dry twigs that alerted Lauder. He'd been sitting in the darkened kitchen for about half an hour, fighting drowsiness and beginning to think he'd got the night wrong, when suddenly there was a slight cry, bringing him bolt upright.

A black shape hobbled in the field midway between the trees and his land, about twenty yards away from the area he'd been watching. As two more sinister figures emerged from behind the stone wall, making to assist the straggler, Lauder felt his mouth drying and his heart begin to race. He took deep breaths, fighting to steady himself, knowing he mustn't panic. He reached for the mobile, telling himself he'd been lucky so far. Clearly he'd been watching the wrong zone. He'd been right about the time they would come, the direction of the approach, but not the exact line. It was fortunate for him somebody had stepped in a rabbit hole, a rut or whatever. The light was so bad out there you almost had to be looking directly at an object before it registered on the retina. But for the stumble his first warning of their presence might have been the sound of a window being forced.

He quickly dialled '999'. Within thirty seconds he had stated the emergency services he required and was connected with the police. He'd anticipated the questions he would be asked so without prompting gave his name and address, then succinctly outlined the threat he faced. The woman at the other end was both well-trained and bright. She didn't interrupt him, and when finished she provided the best therapy for anxiety possible by saying a mobile unit would be immediately despatched to his aid. She then advised him to barricade himself in a room and not confront the burglars.

The first bit of advice was excellent, Lauder thought as he raced through the lounge to take the stairs two at a time. He closed the bedroom door – barricade himself in he would, but as to not confronting them he knew he would have no choice. He inched the wardrobe into place, then slowly lowered it onto its side. He'd spent a sweaty quarter of an hour earlier that evening frog-marching and dragging the solid oak piece across the room. Now with perspiration starting to prickle his forehead again, he stood back to survey his handiwork. He'd got his barricade. It wouldn't keep his visitors out indefinitely but it would certainly slow them down.

A splintering noise followed by a heavy thud announced that he was no longer alone in the house. The sound seemed to come from the downstairs bedroom, which was at the end of the drive and bordered by fields on two sides. So the window there was an obvious candidate for forcing. A filthy expletive and another two thuds from that quarter confirmed his opinion. There followed the sound of doors being jerked open, the hurrying tramp of boots and a couple of bursts of muttered conversation.

Lauder dowsed the small bedside light he'd been working by. The sudden darkness plus the racket of three sets of heavy footsteps now scrambling up the stairs began to unnerve him. He found himself gasping, on the edge of hyperventilation. The messages pounding on his brain were that this time he'd bitten off more than he could chew, that the odds were too unequal, that the reality was much worse than he'd imagined, and more than likely he would spend the rest of his life in a wheelchair.

But the sight of the barricade easily holding the first push saw the onset of his control returning. Amidst a cacophony of blasphemies and curses issuing outside the door, he realised that so far he'd anticipated events and reacted appropriately. He told himself he just needed to remain cool and there was little reason for the pattern to change.

And another way to achieve that, Lauder thought, was to confuse them. Just as an urgent voice, hoarse with effort, demanded from the landing, "C'mon, put your backs into it... then we'll have the bugger," he threw open the window. The pitch of the roof there, dropping down to the lounge wall, was shallower; it could be traversed, working along the dormer, and led to the flat roof serving the study on the west side of the house.

Then, as another tremendous effort was launched on the bedroom door, he sped into the adjacent bathroom. This and the small hatch door, in the corner and to his left, provided his escape route. The gaping window in the other room was bound to divert them – gave him more precious minutes before they realised where he'd gone. He pulled the hatch door open and returned to the bedroom.

Lauder arrived just as another concerted onslaught this time forced the door open a couple of inches. But the carpet had started rucking; and another avalanche of energy failed to enlarge the gap at all.

Again the same voice as before rasped out. Lauder recognised it as Henshaw's, the tone thick with effort and now rage, "See if you can get your hand through to pull the fucking thing down," he ordered. The beam of a flashlight began to play on the offending material.

Lauder reacted immediately. He moved around the upturned wardrobe and side-on to the partially open door. Then as a large hand appeared at the bottom corner and began to scrabble for a purchase on the cloth, he struck. Keeping his eye on the target, conveniently illuminated by the light from the torch, he swung his right leg and kicked downwards. A hideous scream rang out as his toe-end smashed the hand up against the edge of the door.

Tumult erupted on the landing. Against a backdrop of sobbing, ferocious voices swore death and all manner of horrible ends for him. Lauder noisily climbed onto the window sill, then as quietly as he could, crept into the bathroom. He'd been presented with an unexpected opportunity and taken full advantage of it. He suspected he'd broken a couple of fingers on the man's hand, which went some way to lessening the odds against him. But he knew he'd goaded them even more – if there had been a remote chance of being shown leniency, it had disappeared without trace.

Sure enough, to a litany of obscenities, another heart-bursting assault was unleashed on the bedroom door; this time a combined strength, born of fury, was winning. He could hear the wardrobe slowly but relentlessly being pushed back. He quickly entered the roof space and switched on the light. Then he turned and with some difficulty manoeuvred the four-foot high door back into place. The magnetic catches caught, and Lauder swivelled again. He turned off the overhead bulb and using a pencil torch began, half-crouched, to work his way along the boarded catwalk.

He stopped half way along the alley. It was bounded by a wide structural wall on one side and the other was the back of the bedroom. A small hole on his right led through the stonework into the recess above the kitchen. On his left, through the plaster wall, bedlam was occurring. The carpet must have rucked behind the wardrobe this time, and, short of a couple of inches to gain access, the three 'stooges' had developed the strategy of using the door as a battering ram. Accompanied by a crescendo of swearing another splintering crash carried to him, followed by the dragging sound of wood being forced over carpet.

A breathless, hoarse voice exclaimed, "Try getting in, Fred – the bloody gap should be big enough."

So now he knew who he was up against, Lauder grimly thought. That slip in the heat of the moment told all. Henshaw, Kerr and, undoubtedly, Golightly made up the unholy trio. He might have known – they were as thick as thieves, and the ones who would have clamoured most to get at him.

More blasphemies and grunting occurred, all the time attended by the protesting creak of wood upon wood, before the sound of a body half-falling into the room reached Lauder. He extinguished the torch and sat perfectly still. He must do nothing to give away his presence in the loft. Let them get on the roof – waste minutes and energy chasing his red herring. He glanced at the luminous hands of his watch and ended up tapping it to see if it was still working. Incredibly, it was only eleven minutes since he phoned the police. Time had been suspended! It seemed an aeon ago when he first noticed the intruders. And, of course, the sobering thought was that he had at least another twenty minutes to keep ahead or fend them off.

The sound of the wardrobe being manhandled to one side interrupted Lauder's thoughts. Then a coarse voice said, "It looks as if the twat's scarpered out of the window."

Henshaw spoke, the tone peremptory and full of anger. "Take a look outside with the flashlight. He could be hiding at the far side of the dormer or on the flat roof," then, and obviously to the third man: "Get downstairs and have a quick look."

Lauder used the respective sounds of a heavy body clambering onto the window ledge and another hurtling downstairs to squeeze through the opening into the area above the kitchen. Nor was it a moment too soon. For hardly had he got onto the exposed joists when he heard footsteps entering the bathroom. Lauder carefully sat down, his bottom on one beam and his feet on its neighbour. He switched off the torch, knowing what would happen next.

The hatch door was suddenly jerked open and roughly thrown to one side. The light of a powerful torch then illuminated the catwalk and the spot where he'd been a mere thirty seconds before. The beam was played from side to side as Henshaw had a thorough look along the passageway. But he made no attempt to enter.

Lauder remained still. He knew enough of Henshaw to realise he wouldn't act alone. Besides as a pied piper of sorts he wanted all the nasty children to follow him. His wish started to come true with the din of what he thought was Kerr returning from his aerial inspection. There was a thud as the man, presumably, jumped from the window sill. He was talking the second he saw Henshaw, the voice high with frustrated belligerence.

"There's no sign of the cunt...Happen he's worked along the room with the flat roof and got down the fall pipe there."

"Maybe we're meant to think that."

There was a grunt of affirmation, and it wasn't difficult for Lauder to surmise that Henshaw was pointing to the gaping entrance to the loft.

The flashlight once more swept down the length of the catwalk. It was time to move, and quickly. Lauder once more switched his torch back on and began to gingerly cross the joists, heading for the corner of the roof space. The incoming electricity cable went through the kitchen ceiling there, falling to the meter and the junction box below. That was his marker: the cupboard housing the equipment was directly above the kitchen table.

Lauder reached the spot he wanted and momentarily steadied himself by grasping an overhead rafter. They'd heard him! He could hear their jubilation, their filthy comments, as they grunted their way along the catwalk. In a few more steps they would be able to see him. But it no longer mattered – the cat and mouse phase was over and he'd delayed them more than he ever dared hope.

He raised his right leg and rammed it down between the joists. The plaster board cracked on two sides and began to sag ominously. He could hear plaster and debris raining down onto the kitchen floor. It was easy – after all he'd put his foot through a board when tidying the loft three months ago. So why shouldn't he do it when intended? He stamped downwards again, and a large section, complete with yellow insulation, crashed to the floor revealing the table below.

Lauder knelt and grasped a beam on either side. He started to lower himself through the opening. A bellow of rage, uglier because of the confined space, rang out. He turned halfway down, and though partially blinded by the flashlight saw the hooded figure of one of the thugs lunge from the catwalk exit toward him. He let himself down to his full length and, flexing his legs, dropped a yard to the table top. He landed quite softly, the table rocked fractionally but stayed upright. Then he was on the ground and yanking the table away from the hole above it.

Torchlight accompanied by heavy breathing and much swearing flooded down from the broken ceiling. "Christ!" Kerr exclaimed furiously. "The crazy cunt must have dropped about twelve feet. I tell you, I don't bloody well fancy that!"

"Back, back!" Henshaw's voice almost screamed.

Heavy feet thudded on the beams; a section of the ceiling near the kitchen door sagged alarmingly then cracked. Lauder picked up the cudgel he'd left next to the table and raced into the lounge. He snatched a glance at his watch; it was now eighteen minutes since he put in the call to the police. Twelve minutes at least to keep the thugs at bay.

Thugs – a plural of three! Where was Golightly? He hadn't heard his voice in the loft. Was the man out of it – nursing his injured hand with no appetite left for the fight? Or was he back with the others? Or even worse still, acting alone? Panic once more threatened to engulf Lauder, scrambling his thoughts. He felt his earlier ascendancy slipping, the imponderables crowding in on him with no ready answers forthcoming. But as thunderous footfalls resounded from the upstairs rooms he fought to resist it – breathing deeply, telling himself what he must do next.

He dragged the heavy wooden coffee table to within two yards of the lounge door. Then with a last look round the room to establish his line of retreat, he flicked off the torch and waited. A picture flashed through his mind of Aldershot nearly forty years ago. A windswept parade ground and a red-faced NCO bawling at them, "An enemy running at you isn't frightening, it's the stuff of sweet dreams. What did I say?" he demanded. "It's the stuff of sweet dreams, sergeant," they'd echoed.

"And why? I'll tell you why – because he's supplying

two thirds of the energy you're going to hit him with. It's like two cars crashing head on – very nasty. Hit a man like that and he won't ever like you again!"

The door was wrenched open, and a menacing, broad shouldered figure burst into the room. Lauder reacted instantly from a half crouched position; he pivoted and slammed home a right handed punch into Kerr's midriff. There was a terrible groan, the man's flashlight thudded to the ground and he collapsed to his knees.

Henshaw nearly got to Lauder. He'd glimpsed his accelerating shape, baseball bat upraised, a few yards behind Kerr. But the man's momentum, plus the sudden absence of torchlight, proved his undoing. His feet encountered Kerr's legs and he too went down.

Lauder rapidly stepped round the coffee table, putting it between himself and Henshaw. The ploy worked. In the dimness of the room where the only light now was from the display panel on the video recorder, the man either didn't see the obstacle or was too distracted to see it. Swearing dreadfully, Henshaw recovered his feet and, baseball bat poised, sprang towards him. His shins heavily collided with the table edge, and for the second time he fell with wooden legs splintering and breaking beneath him. That was Lauder's cue, and hefting his own club, he moved in on Henshaw to smash it down on the man's outstretched leg. Solid wood impacted bone and an awful scream began reverberating around the room.

A vicious oath penetrated the din. Lauder turned unbelievingly to see Kerr rising from his knees. He couldn't credit it – he thought he'd put the thug out of action for at least a few minutes. He took to his heels. He realised he couldn't afford to get embroiled in a close-quarters fight with someone like Kerr. The man was just too tough and strong. Lauder, at his age, had no illusions. He knew it just needed one solid blow from the brawler and he'd have the stuffing knocked out of him, and then he'd be in the worst straits of his life!

Lauder streaked through the hall and jerked open the

door to the porch. He'd damaged them all now – slowed them down. And the final phase was ahead of him. In a running battle outdoors, they'd find him even more elusive, and the minutes to the cavalry arriving were ticking away. Dare he hope he was on the brink of doing it?

He emerged from the porch, locked the door and pocketed the key. That would baulk them a bit longer, he reckoned. He'd made perhaps two yards towards the garage when suddenly his shoulders were grasped and he was wrenched round. Golightly, Lauder despairingly thought, just as the blur of a hooded head exploded in his face.

Blood jetting from both nostrils, his legs turning to jelly, Lauder staggered back. The murkiness of the night had now been transformed to a kaleidoscope of brightly coloured stars – as one lot fizzled out an equally brilliant set of replacements would burst into life. His feet met an obstacle and he fell heavily into a sitting position. He dimly realised he'd lurched backwards across the width of the drive and was now sprawling beside his lawn roller against the garage wall.

Everything seemed to be happening in slow motion. He saw the indistinct figure of Golightly, framed by an array of shooting stars, advancing towards him. The kennel-man was swinging a wooden club in his one good hand, plainly readying to deliver more punishment. Lauder cursed himself. He hadn't known where Golightly was – somehow preferred to think he was out of the fight – and now he was going to pay terribly!

The small multi-coloured explosions began to subside. Lauder grasped the shaft of the roller and painfully pulled himself up a few inches as Golightly loomed over him. Despite the gloom he could see the man's left hand was bound by a white handkerchief, while the other was bringing the club erect.

Lauder rammed the roller handle forward with all the force he could muster. The solid wooden 'T' piece of the five-foot long shaft, gathering speed, crashed into the base of the man's throat. Golightly dropped his club. Both his good hand and his injured one flew to his neck. He made an awful strangulated cry and teetered on his feet.

There was no second invitation needed by Lauder. He dragged himself to his feet and with the best of his dwindling strength sank a short jab into Golightly's solar plexus. The man involuntarily began to double over under the impact of the second blow. Only for a third blow, provided by Lauder's knee driving upwards, to arrest the process by smashing home on his jaw. Lauder stood trembling, gasping for air, as the kennel man fell to his knees and then slumped to the ground.

Meanwhile Henshaw and Kerr, unaware of the vicious struggle enacted mere yards away, were wrestling with the porch door. Kerr, beside himself with rage, swearing horribly, suddenly lashed out with his baseball bat to shatter the oblong of glass set in the top part of the door.

"What's the point of that, you dummy!" Henshaw snarled, his voice racked with pain. "It's too small to get out of."

"I fucking well felt better, didn't I!" Kerr shouted, wide-eyed and glaring at him.

Henshaw shook his head. "Get a bloody grip on yourself, will you," he cried, then started back into the hall. "C'mon, there's a door in the lounge, or we'll get out the way we came."

He limped laboriously into the kitchen. Things had got totally out of hand, he sourly thought. So far they'd taken a mauling from that bastard, Lauder, and not one of them had been able to put so much as a glove on him. He stopped at a set of switches and flicked on the outside light along with those for the lounge. His hand instinctively strayed down to his right knee. It was throbbing and swelling even as he explored. He didn't think there was anything broken, but the slightest movement was excruciating.

A string of obscenities greeted Henshaw as he dragged

himself into the lounge, Evidently the patio door was locked and there was no sign of a key. A fuming Kerr raced past him to disappear towards the downstairs bedroom. He hobbled after him.

Henshaw glanced at his watch – it was now over twenty minutes since they'd broken in. Far too long! It was all going horribly wrong, he chafed. He'd planned to be in and out within ten minutes. Lauder must have phoned the police, so they were on the edge of serious trouble. They should quit now – cut their losses and get out fast. But the problem was Kerr. He was completely out of control. He'd heard talk before but never realised the full extent of what he was like. The man had been angry up till the time Lauder had whacked him. But in the last five minutes he'd been behaving like a madman. He'd somehow have to get a rein on him. He groaned – Golightly had some influence over Kerr. But where the hell was he?

He arrived at the gaping dining room window. There was no sign of Kerr. He pushed the damaged frame open even further and managed to hoist himself onto the window sill. Grunting with effort and distress, he pulled his knees up then swivelled to project his legs through the opening. He squirmed forward in a sitting position until his limbs were hanging down next to the outer wall. This was the tricky bit, he nervously thought. He had to launch himself with his good leg leading to drop the two feet to the flagged path below. He did exactly as he intended. His left leg touched the ground first, taking his body's weight. But within a couple of inches of getting his other leg down and stabilising himself, he skidded. It was probably a thin film of moisture lying on the stone flags, was his last tangible thought. Then his mind was consumed by a searing agony as he collapsed in a heap with his injured leg taking the full force of the fall.

A harrowing cry reached Lauder as he arrived at the edge of the wood. He looked back and saw a menacing figure, wearing a gaudy ski-mask, appear in the pool of illumination provided by the outside light. The man spotted the prostrate shape of Golightly and moved quickly to bend over him.

Lauder found his second club and wearily entered the trees. It was definitely not Kerr who was suffering, he grimly thought. The man was walking easily and looked frighteningly formidable. So it had to be Henshaw, somewhere in the background, who'd aggravated his injury. The odds were lessening, but in his present condition that was now scant consolation.

He snatched a look at his wristwatch and saw it was nearly thirty minutes since he rang the police. If he could hold out a little longer he might just win through, he told himself. His tactics now though had to be very different. The hit and run phase was finished, as was the possibility of fleeing – his options were strictly limited.

Just as he'd anticipated, the fight had taken a considerable toll. The physical evidence, apart from one nostril which was still streaming blood, wasn't alarming. But Lauder felt exhausted. The resilience he'd once prided himself on, to take hard knocks and still keep going, was totally absent. His head ached badly and his body felt drained of all energy. He'd barely been able to climb the stone wall a few minutes ago.

From the sanctuary of the trees, Lauder looked fearfully back towards Kerr. The man seemed to have done what he could to help his friend Golightly, and was now, flashlight in hand, squatting in the middle of the drive eyeing his surroundings. He knew he could no longer face the thug on anything like equal terms. In fact, having already sampled Kerr's toughness, he realised he wouldn't have been able to cope with him under normal circumstances. He had to hide – it was the only course open to him. There were heavy branches and a few fallen trees lying in the wood; one of them was bound to provide the cover he so sorely needed.

Lauder glanced anxiously behind him as he worked deeper into the trees, Kerr was moving and, ominously, must have decided that the wood was where his hunting would be best rewarded. The man, flashlight swaying in front of him, was crossing the lawn heading for the boundary wall more or less on the line he'd taken. Eyes skinned, trying not to make a sound, Lauder lengthened his stride.

In the dim light filtering down from the quarter moon, the fallen tree looked ideal. It lay square on to anyone approaching from the house, was thick enough to conceal him, and with a small bush growing about seven feet away from the mushroom of its root system, gave cover on both sides. Lauder stepped over the trunk and lowered himself to the ground.

A huge feeling of relief swept over him. He lay face pressed up to the bark, almost hugging the contour of the tree. The refuge was even better than he had first gauged: with the root bowl at his feet and the low bush just beyond his head, Kerr would nearly have to stand on him before he could be seen. And with help imminent the odds of that happening had to be incredibly long.

He risked a peep, and was the next moment recoiling in horror. Kerr, flashlight pointing down at the ground, was about ten yards away and coming directly towards him. It couldn't be accidental – how could the man know so unerringly where he was? Lauder's hand flopped from his sweating brow to rest on the wind-cheater he wore, and suddenly the answer was terrorising his mind. He'd left a trail just as surely as taking part in a paper-chase. His hand was wet with blood. It had been dripping from his nose unchecked because there'd been no time to stem the flow. Then to exacerbate the matter, his coat – made of a water resistant fabric – rather than absorbing the blood had simply deflected it onto the ground. Little wonder Kerr had made a bee-line for him. Under the flashlight's beam there was a glistening path which even someone half blind could follow.

Kerr was quite close now. Even lying pressed up to the fallen trunk he was registering flashes of reflected light from the trees and undergrowth nearby. Again he steeled himself, pushing back those waves of panic that had persistently tried to overcome him in the last half hour. One last supreme effort, he told himself, then with the police getting even nearer he might just make it. He determined to stay where he was instead of rising to confront the thug. He tensed and grasped his club more firmly. Kerr just had to stick his ugly face over the log and he would find he wasn't beaten yet.

A twig snapped and there was a rustle of dry leaves being disturbed. Lauder could hear the man's breathing, and the flashlight's beam was now streaming over the trunk a mere foot above his head. It could only mean that Kerr was almost upon him and readying himself for an attack. He felt like screaming so great was the strain; his mouth was bone dry and the sound of his heart deafening.

Suddenly, amazingly, the thin column of white light switched through ninety degrees. Lauder heard footsteps moving away from him in the direction of the tree's base. Then close to the bowl of the root system the beam turned back at right angles. He snatched a look; and unbelievable though it seemed, there was Kerr about six yards adjacent to him moving deeper into the wood. He jerked his head round, back into near contact with the surface of the trunk. There was no way he was going to allow the blur of a white face to squander his miraculous reprieve. He huddled his length along the tree, not moving a muscle.

A coarse sneering voice said, "Did you think I'd give you a second chance to tag me, cunt?" He was bathed in the flashlight's harsh beam, and the miraculous reprieve was over as suddenly as it had begun.

Lauder scrambled to his feet and stepped backwards over the log. Kerr was perhaps five yards off, advancing inexorably on him. The man threw his flashlight to one side and gripped the baseball bat he'd been carrying with two hands.

"You can run, rabbit but this time there's no place to hide," the thug growled.

"I'd never run from trash like you.," Lauder said with a

conviction he didn't feel as he stumbled backwards. His one hastily formed thought was to find the open and then goad the man into a mistake.

Kerr laughed contemptuously then suddenly sprang forward, swinging the baseball bat. Lauder saw the trajectory of the swipe and just managed to block the blow. The sheer force of it though, sent him staggering backwards. He half-collided with a tree, glanced off and then was defending himself again. A pattern emerged with Lauder being driven back, and never far from losing his feet under a hail of full-blooded blows.

He lurched into the field, and Kerr was on him again. The man aimed and with two hands took a tremendous swipe at his head. Lauder just brought his staff up in time. There was a resounding crack as wood crashed into wood, and then he was empty-handed.

Lauder half-turned to look sickly at what had been his defence rolling in two pieces on the turf behind him. Terror gripped him. His breath was coming in gasps as he felt on the point of gibbering. He wanted a hole to open up and swallow him, to sprout wings and fly... anything to distance himself from the fiend now closing in on him.

"I don't need this to settle the hash of a cunt like you," Kerr announced and, astoundingly, hurled the baseball bat across the field.

The moon had reappeared and in the silvery light Lauder saw the white gash of a mean grin. Plainly the thug was relishing the situation, he thought, a vestige of hope returning. He'd sized up his weakened condition, decided it was a non-contest and was itching to give him a savage beating.

'BBC', the sergeant major used to scream at them. They'd be in sweating pairs, locked in unarmed combat, and he'd bawl his slogan in their ears as he patrolled amongst them. Balls, belly and chin the letters stood for – the bodily parts which when hit thoroughly could stop a man in his tracks... Lauder's choice was the chin. He closed, feinted with his left and threw a right cross. The second the punch connected he knew he was lost. Whether Kerr had moved slightly at the last moment, whether sapped as he was his coordination had deteriorated, whether it was the poor light, or a combination of all three, the blow landed two inches above the jaw to the side of the man's ear. It was bread and butter to a brawler like Kerr, the thug merely grunted and shook his head.

The next moment a meaty fist crashed onto Lauder's right temple. His legs became feeble and his senses began to swim. He instinctively covered up, trying to move inside Kerr's reach. But an excruciatingly painful elbow to the ribs followed by a lip ripping uppercut to the mouth convinced him of the lunacy of the tactic, and he stumbled away.

Kerr pursued him, delivering a torrent of blows. There was nothing scientific about the way the thug fought, Lauder dimly thought, as he tried to protect himself as best he could. The man bludgeoned his opponent; so strong was he that even a glancing blow hurt and damaged. A particularly heavy punch found a gap in his guard, exploding on his jaw, and with the sky wheeling and vortexing above him, Kerr's muscular figure dissolving and reforming in front of him, he went down.

A rough pair of hands reached down, fastened his coat and yanked him to his feet. Semi-conscious, his resistance totally gone, he was dragged a few yards and thrust up against a tree. Then with powerful arms pinning him to the trunk, Kerr's forehead smashed into his face.

Teetering on the edge of oblivion, real dread possessed Lauder. Despite the awful pain, his evaporating senses, a corner of his mind shrieked at the awful plight he was in. This grunting, tobacco-reeking brute assaulting him was a maniac. The man knew no dividing line – completely lacked any semblance of normal discretion. Lauder realised when he went down – as he surely must in the next few seconds – he would be systematically kicked to a pulp.

Another terrible blow crashed home on Lauder's jaw

and he lost consciousness. Even Kerr's restraining arm couldn't hold his collapsing dead weight and he slithered down the length of the man's frame. He momentarily came out of the black void to see the array of brightly coloured shooting stars he'd seen earlier. His body uncoiled along the damp grass, and amidst the roaring in his ears, the incandescence of the scene before him, astonishingly, there was Ben lolloping towards him. Something thudded heavily onto the ground next to him as he passed out again.

Aileen threw the baseball bat away as if it were a snake. She rushed past Kerr's prostrate body and flung herself next to Lauder. Tears began to rain uncontrollably down her cheeks as she saw the extent of his injuries. She leant forward to cradle the gory head, cursing the monster lying behind her and then herself. If only she'd acted sooner, she railed, then Iain might have been spared this terrible ordeal.

As soon as she saw the grey bulk of the Land Rover parked in the lay-by next to the main road, alarm bells had started blaring. The fact that the vehicle was there in such a solitary spot at twenty minutes before one in the morning, was suspicious. But when she established from the registration plate it didn't belong to anyone in the village, the implications assumed nightmarish proportions.

Ben must have thought he was out for a run. Fear propelled her feet; within five minutes she'd raced the length of the road to the turn-off and climbed the small hill leading up to Iain's house. Even before it came into view she finally knew something was wrong, terribly wrong. The place was lit up like a pleasure park. The outside lamp was on and there was light being shed from at least three of the downstairs rooms. On the edge of panic, Aileen reached the entrance and sped down the drive.

The window of the porch door was smashed. There was a hooded man half sprawled up against the garage wall. Then to her horror another sinister figure limped painfully from the far corner of the house. He saw her standing, clutching Ben's collar, then hastily ducked back out of view.

A grunt, immediately followed by an awful groan, reached her ears. She turned to see two dark shapes forty yards away at the edge of the wood. An anguished cry left Aileen's lips, for the smaller of the two, the man being mercilessly beaten, had the unmistakable build and posture of Iain.

Aileen couldn't remember what happened next. She had no recollection of running the intervening distance, scaling the garden wall or what she intended. What did remain in her mind was the oval of Iain's mouth over the thug's shoulder, the lips drawn away from the teeth in agony as yet another terrible blow smashed into him. She kicked the baseball bat in her headlong rush, skidded to a stop, scooped it up and struck with all her might. The brute, so involved in his bestial work, had no inkling of danger until the club crashed home above his left ear, and he dropped, pole-axed.

"Get a hold of yourself, get a hold of yourself!" Aileen demanded of herself.

She ran a hand across her face wiping away the tears. It was no time for women's vapours, she roughly told herself. She must help Iain, and quickly. In the light of her little torch, his injuries looked even worse under close examination. His face was a gory mask of devastation. The right eye was a bulbous mess, already purple and so swollen a mere slit represented the presence of an eyeball. Blood gushed from one nostril; and a three inch long gash, running from his upper lip to a horribly distended left cheek, was bubbling and foaming every time he exhaled. Alarmed he might begin choking she started to tug and pull his body into a sideways position as gently as she could.

Aileen looked wildly around as two police cars, blue lights flashing, crunched down the drive. Four officers spilled out with the biggest, a sergeant – and the one she was sure Iain had described to her – giving the orders. The man turned, hearing her frantic calls, and with another policeman hard on his heels, raced towards her.

Sergeant Young listened gravely to Aileen's brief but halting account of what had happened. Kneeling beside her above the unconscious Lauder, he didn't interrupt. His only action was to put a reassuring hand on her shoulder at one point when the emotion she was so visibly trying to suppress seemed about to overcome her. Then no sooner had he grasped the essence of the situation than he plunged into action.

First to the constable with him and pointing at Kerr, who was now swearing and growling his way back to full consciousness. "Right, cuff that animal and we'll put him in the second car as soon as he's fit to walk."

Then shouting across to the elder of the two policemen accompanying a limping Henshaw and a befuddled Golightly towards the vehicles: "Ron, get on the phone to the hospital and have them send an ambulance straight away."

Finally he turned back to Aileen, his voice immediately modulating. "There may be internal bleeding, Mrs Carter, so we'd best not move him," he said quietly. "What we've got to do in the next twenty minutes until the ambulance arrives is see he loses as little body heat as possible. We need some blankets, and whatever else from the house which will help."

Aileen nodded. "I know where they're kept," she said to Young, her eyes reluctantly leaving Lauder for a moment.

The sergeant glanced at the fresh-faced officer next to him. "Constable Gore will look after him, Mrs Carter," he said, "and we'll just be a few minutes."

The eldest of Young's squad, some grey hair straying from beneath his cap, met them as they hurried onto the drive.

"The ambulance is on its way, Sarge," he said, and then indicating Golightly slumped in the back seat of the car, "and that one has got a broken hand."

A fleeting glint of satisfaction appeared in Young's eyes. "Put friend Kerr in with the others, and you and Eric better run them to outpatients. Then I'll see you back at the station. And, Ron," he said beginning to turn away, "get on the blower again – I want the scene of crime people out of bed and here soonest."

He crossed the drive to join Mrs Carter who was unlocking the front door. She'd said there was a store of blankets in the upstairs bedroom. They crunched through the broken glass in the porch, passed underneath the gaping hole in the kitchen ceiling and picked their way round the wreckage of what had once been a coffee table in the lounge. Then they climbed the stairs to find a splintered bedroom door hanging askew from one hinge. But it was at the sight of the scoured and cracked wardrobe beyond that the woman's thinly-held composure broke. Young heard a tiny cry, and when he looked he saw her stifling sobs and tears splashing down her cheeks.

What it must have been like! Aileen despairingly thought, the sergeant's sympathetic hand on her shoulder no solace at all. What sort of people were they? In his own house, they'd put him at bay. Smashed, destroyed, ruined everything in their path to get at him. What terror, desperation Iain must have experienced. She vainly tried to stem the flow of tears with the cuff of her jacket as she pulled three thick blankets from the box.

"I've seen it too," Young said gently. "They'll pay, don't worry, I'll guarantee it."

"They'd better, sergeant," Aileen cried, her cheeks wet and suffused with anger. "If they're not punished, and severely, I for one won't be responsible for my future actions." She raced past him and began to descend the stairs.

The young policeman was craning over Lauder when they returned. He glanced at the sergeant and then at Aileen. "I think he's coming round," he said, the relief in his voice evident. "He stirred and his eyes fluttered just a few seconds ago."

"OK," Young stated, "the main heat loss will be from below so let's first get a blanket underneath him. But we must be careful to move him as little as possible."

Aileen nodded, folded one of the blankets and then knelt down to spread it alongside Lauder's body. Lauder felt himself struggling out of a deep, dark well. There was light at the top of the formless hole and a jumble of incoherent voices amidst the hubbub drumming in his ears. He saw a blur of flashing blue lights and decided he was on the brink of another firework display. Then as reason began to assert itself he realised there were police cars standing on the drive.

A devil was in operation on his left side, working from within, a little fiend, travelling round his rib cage and well versed in inflicting agony. It would drive home a razor sharp dagger and then attack another spot with excruciating results. Strong hands grasped him, moving him sideways, and the devil intensified its efforts. He passed out.

"He's slipped away again," Young observed. He picked up the brandy decanter and glass he'd grabbed in his rush back through the house. "Some of this can only help."

"I'll do it," Aileen said, reaching out for the Martell. "And could one of you seek some hot water and towels, please."

Young glanced at the constable and inclined his head towards the house. The young man hurried off, Aileen pulled a blanket over Lauder and carefully tucked it around him. In the light of the torch she had to steel herself once more as she bent over him. The lower left side of his face had ballooned up even further in the short time she'd been away, indicating the jaw was broken; his right eye was now totally closed, and the horrible gash travelling diagonally up from his lip was still weeping blood. She trickled her fingers in the brandy and tried to steer a little into his mouth, again fighting tears as she did so.

A few drops entered his gullet and suddenly Lauder was spluttering back to consciousness. His one good eye opened, focused, and the next moment a parody of a crooked smile appeared on his blood-splattered, grimy face.

"Hello, flower… it's you – how marvellous!" he croaked, the words almost inaudible.

It was too much for Aileen. A great sob escaped her body, then another. She lunged for his hand, ineffectually trying to brush away tears with the other.

Lauder groaned as another spasm of pain racked his body. "God," he said faintly. "It seems I bit off a bit more than I could chew."

Young darted a look at Aileen, then down to Lauder. "What's that mean?" he asked sharply.

If Lauder heard the question he ignored it. To him Young's substantial frame towering above him was an irrelevancy. His one functional eye remained fixed on Aileen. She was all that mattered – at that time no-one else existed. He squeezed her hand, his fingers searching and interlocking with hers.

Amidst the sea of pain, the horror of what had been, she was a lifeline. He felt should he once release her he would plunge once more into that abyss of darkness.

The hot water and the towels arrived in the shape of Constable Gore with Ben, his new-found friend, trotting beside him. And Aileen, seemingly unfazed by the inconvenience of having only one hand free, began to gently sponge away the worst of the dirt and congealed blood from Lauder's face.

Young, with Gore standing beside him, watched with silent fascination as the cleansing progressed; the woman and the injured man joined as if by an umbilical cord through which he was receiving the strength and care he so badly needed. He knew he and Gore might as well be on another planet so unaware were the pair of their presence. She only broke off her ministering when the distress became too great, when Lauder was gasping and moaning with the force of it. Then, still holding and being held by one hand, she was bending forward inches above his face, murmuring endearments, caressing, sometimes kissing him, until the worst of the pain had passed.

It was the same when the ambulance, klaxon wailing and lights flashing, slowed to a halt five minutes later. Lauder would simply not release his woman's hand. The two paramedics had to make a quick examination, an injection to his bottom and transfer him to the stretcher, all without disturbing the apparently unbreakable bond of their entwined hands. Young followed the stretcher bearers and Mrs Carter. He saw them negotiate their way through a large break in the stone wall, which was due to Gore's sterling efforts of a few moments before. Then it was across the lawn, the arms connection still intact, to the waiting ambulance.

Two minutes later Young watched as the vehicle's tail lights disappeared from the drive. He turned to Gore standing next to him. "Well, lad," he said, "that's love for you...I swear if he hadn't been so banged about they would have been shagging by now."

CHAPTER TEN

Aileen came out of a deep sleep as the discordant sound of the alarm clock filled the room. She grumbled and stretched an arm out to switch off the noise; it was just after eleven o clock. She rose, dressed quickly with jeans and sweater, washed and then went downstairs.

Ben raised himself in his basket, tail thumping, as she entered the kitchen. She would have to ask June, next door, to look after him for a few hours this afternoon, she thought, fondling his head and ears. It had been made quite clear last night that dogs, even ones with Ben's pleasant disposition, were not welcome in the antiseptic environment of the hospital. She gave him a meal and then set about preparing some poached eggs and toast for herself.

Aileen sat down at the table and started chewing thoughtfully. She felt jaded and drained after the trials and shocks of last night. But gradually the therapeutic effect of food on an empty stomach began to make her feel better.

It had been well after five this morning when she returned home; with the first fingers of light showing in the eastern sky she'd been driven back to the village in a police car, which Sergeant Young had considerately detoured for her. Prior to that, she'd spent two stressful and lonely hours in the waiting room of the accident and emergency department.

The tolerance shown by the paramedics had been replaced by the cool professionalism of two young doctors on their arrival at hospital. Iain's hand was separated from hers and she was kindly but pointedly told of the availability of a coffee machine in the waiting room. There she fretted and worried for what seemed an age; her only companion for a time a mumbling drunk, who'd broken an arm in his excesses earlier in the night, and, suitably doctored, was waiting for a lift from his luckless brother-in-law.

Eventually one of the two registrars had come to her. Aileen remembered first thinking that the weary young man in front of her could be no more than her son's age. Then that being immediately replaced by an enormous relief as the white-faced doctor pushed back a recalcitrant lock of black hair and told her there were no complications they could uncover with Iain's condition.

The intelligent eyes had studied her for a moment. "Of course, it's just as well," he said, "because Mr Lauder's been thoroughly knocked about. Besides the bog-standard cuts and bruises, he's got three broken ribs, a fractured jaw and a broken finger in his right hand."

Aileen nodded dumbly, temporarily unable to speak, the lump in her throat growing by the second once more.

"It wouldn't have anything to do with the mob the police brought in about half an hour before Mr Lauder arrived?" the doctor asked. "Two of them needed some treatment before they could be taken into custody."

"It would, doctor," Aileen said vehemently. "'Animals' is too good a word to describe them."

The young man shook his head, reflectively. "We live in violent times," he said "I had no idea how until I got this job four months ago."

"Can I see him?" Aileen asked.

She paused now in the act of raising the tea cup to her mouth, remembering how there was something infinitely heart-rending in seeing the person you loved hospitalised for the first time. The doctor had led her to one of the four ante-rooms at the head of the ward reserved for new admissions. He was murmuring words to the effect that she could only stay a few minutes; that Mr Lauder was sedated and his condition stable so there was no cause for alarm. But again she was shocked to the core at the sight of her man. This time he was completely different to the bloodied, grimy figure whose head she'd cradled a few hours ago. The whiteness of the scene shrieked at her. The freshly-laundered sheets drawn up to the drip-white face, the cocoon of bandages round the head; even the metal collar supporting his jaw was sheathed in white plastic.

The helplessness, the vulnerability, somehow emphasised by the plasma drip feeding into Iain's arm, had traumatised her. She began reeling, a cry escaped her throat and but for the young doctor gripping and guiding her to a nearby chair she would have fallen.

"Put your head down and between your knees," he commanded. Then to a nurse who appeared at the room door: "Bring a glass of water, and quickly will you, Alice."

She sipped the ice-cold water, beginning to recover, her eyes fixed on the comatose figure in the bed.

"Too many shocks in too little a time," the nurse said sympathetically. "But don't worry – he may look awful but he's strong and is going to be all right."

Aileen glanced gratefully at her before murmuring "It was just a blow to see him like that."

"I know," the woman replied, "sometimes a patient in recovery looks worse than at the time of the accident."

The registrar, who'd slipped out of the room for a couple of minutes, reappeared. He took her pulse and cast a professional eye over her.

"A good sleep is what you need, Mrs Carter," he pronounced. "The police have just been on the phone. Apparently there's a car heading out your way on a routine matter, and they're happy to give you a lift. It will be here in a few minutes."

Aileen picked up the dishes and moved to the sink. She ran hot water, reflecting that the uneventful journey back to the village had ended what was without doubt the worst night of her life.

*

Sergeant Young, dressed casually in a grey lamb's wool sweater and dark blue pants, moved through the hatch of the big reception desk at the police station. He acknowledged the duty officer there and walked into the small office behind. This was his domain, what he regarded as the seat of his appreciable power and control within the station. He wasn't responsible for CID, of course, but knew perfectly well that without his information-gathering service and the back-up his uniformed men gave them when required, the plain-clothes boys couldn't function.

He often did this; spent a couple of unscheduled hours between shift changes to put jobs to bed as he called it. It didn't always suit his wife, Brenda, to see him returning to work when he was supposed to be on leave for the next three days. But by now she was largely conditioned to his behaviour. She was a copper's wife, a fine lass, and being the sensible sort he was he intended to take her out that evening for a spanking good dinner.

The truth was, since the two boys had left home he found he got even more satisfaction from his work. He knew he had the respect of his men and it stretched to the top in the shape of DI Moran. He'd never wanted to do anything else. His parents had been regular churchgoers – decent people, and while the habit had never fully taken hold with him, he and his brother had emerged from adolescence sharing much of their values. John had gone into the probation service; whereas he, less clever but tall and sturdy, saw the police force as a natural progression. Right from the start he'd enjoyed the work of the uniformed branch. It was more definite, he was dealing with offences as well as crime. Not for him the riddles thrown up by a crooked accountant or a seven-day-old corpse in a ditch. He didn't kid himself – he couldn't cope with those sorts of complications. He was through and through a law enforcer, and had become good at it. He'd made sergeant eleven years ago, and was now the senior man of the two deployed at the station.

But Young wasn't happy with himself over the Lauder case. He knew he hadn't been entirely discreet when he talked to Driggs after the fracas at the farm. God knows, by now, he should be accustomed to people breaking the law and then putting two fingers up to the police. But the way Lauder covered himself, leaving him powerless to proceed, had rankled. He'd been judgemental, said too much and therefore not conducted himself in his usual professional manner.

In any event, what he thought would lead to Lauder eventually getting a thick ear or his flower beds trampled had turned out very differently indeed. A small vicious war with the man at the receiving end had erupted in the countryside last night. Young, of course, knew that the root of the trouble was that the local huntsmen were still killing foxes. He also knew there was precious little he could do about it. He simply didn't have the men to spare. What with the cuts in manning and resources due to the economic crisis, it needed all his ingenuity just to service the towns and villages of the upper Tyne valley, let alone the huge open spaces of West Northumberland. A few token gestures, such as sending a car to wherever the Hunt where gathering, was the most he could extend to.

Young stretched out his long legs and looked thoughtfully at the wall; seasoned though he was even he had been shaken by the violence last night. As a private individual he'd been largely neutral about the hunting issue, but now he was beginning to wonder if what he'd seen was a sample of the way the Hunt behaved in the field; if so then the horror stories which the activists put out must be grounded in fact.

And it wasn't as if some fringe element was responsible for the extremism. Henshaw was the Master, for crying out loud. Young could barely credit it. The man had seemed rooted in respectability – the town's butcher, a pillar of the Chamber of Commerce, and only recently he'd seen him on TV speaking authoritively as the leader of the Hunt. The little he knew of him he didn't care for. On the few occasions they'd spoken, Henshaw had struck him as sour and uncompromising. But that apart he had never for a minute thought the man would some day be occupying one of his cells.

However, Kerr was altogether a different kettle of fish

– he was no surprise. He was a habitual offender and had been known to them for a long time. A thoroughly nasty piece of work, was Kerr. He was dangerous; anybody had only to be around him for a few minutes to sense that. And if Mrs Carter hadn't pluckily clocked him one when she did, Young very much doubted that Lauder would now be recovering in the local hospital.

He fingered the papers on the rather untidy desk in front of him. The charge sheets promised full reading: assault, malicious damage, breaking and entering, causing an affray, plus grievous bodily harm for Kerr. Mrs Carter had said she would drop by in half an hour, and as for Lauder, well, the hospital had squashed any chance of getting a statement from him before the weekend was over. Nevertheless, Young mused, glancing at another sheaf of hand written notes, they still had plenty of evidence with which to proceed. The scene of the crime report showed quite conclusively the fingerprints of the three were all over the Lauder house.

Young smoothed down his short black hair and stood up. He thought he would pay Mr Kerr a visit in the cells and see how he was enjoying his stay. They'd had their eye on Fred for some time in connection with other matters, and now he was so deep in the mire, the turd might want to do some trading. With a slight grin marking his ruddy face, he entered the reception area, selected a bunch of keys from the rack on the back wall and turned right down a dimly lit passage.

*

Aileen sat at the far side of the desk coolly regarding the man in the expensive, light blue suit who was gesticulating behind it. She'd already discovered the consultant had a taste for cricketing metaphors and now she was being subjected to another.

The doctor, his genial face sunburnt and his dark hair silvering at the temples, was leaning forward. "Mr

Lauder's begun to make a good recovery," he said. "He was on a sticky wicket but we've helped him over that patch."

Aileen was still tired and nervy. The feeling of well-being she'd enjoyed at breakfast had proved temporary; it had dissipated on the journey into the hospital. She supposed it was to be expected – a natural repercussion to the awful events of last night. And now her patience was rapidly evaporating as she listened to the affected blandishments of the dapper man facing her.

"We?" she retorted. "I didn't see you about last night when my fiancé so badly needed treatment."

An indulgent smile appeared on the consultant's face. It read: best ignore the woman's outburst, after all the poor creature has been through a lot in the last twenty-four hours. He switched the conversation.

"Mr Lauder's been asking for you," he said brightly. "I'll take you along there now."

Aileen rose from her chair feeling somewhat ashamed. Her comment, born of irritation, hadn't been justified. Dr Stringfellow, because he was in charge of the accident and emergency unit, wouldn't be serving two masters. A good proportion of his peers on the surgical side would deserve the sort of remark she'd just made. Many of the orthopaedic surgeons, cardiologists, anaesthetists, were so involved with private lists that the pressure placed on their teams, and the senior registrars in particular, manifested itself in longer waiting times. Add to that their almost pathological penchant for professional individualism, which so far had thwarted much standardisation of best surgical practice, and it wasn't difficult to identify a sizeable contributory factor to the problems of the NHS.

She reached the door of Iain's room and offered her hand to the doctor. "I'm sorry I was a bit tetchy before," she said, "and can I thank you for the fine team you've moulded around you."

"I appreciate that, Mrs Carter," the man replied, clasping her hand. "And you can rest assured we'll continue to play it down the middle."

Iain had heard the exchange, and was waiting with a lop-sided grin as she entered the room.

"Oh, darling!" Aileen exclaimed, rushing to the bed with a bunch of tulips leading the charge. She just checked herself in time and, rather than falling into his arms, planted a kiss on his forehead. "How do you feel now?" she asked, bending over him.

Lauder spoke deliberately, like a ventriloquist, his lips barely moving, his difficulty in enunciating quite evident, so firmly was his jaw supported. "As if I've been through a mangle," he muttered. He gave another crooked grin. "But then I have, but worse."

Aileen examined him closely, not saying anything for a moment. The swelling above the jaw fracture on the left side of his face seemed as pronounced as she'd seen. His right eye was still fully closed, the area swollen and a hideous yellowish-purple hue. However, the parchment-white mask of last night had gone, his face having regained a little colour.

Lauder sought her hand with his unbandaged one and gave it a squeeze. "That PC Gore called about nine this morning," he said. "But the medical equivalent to Richie Benaud along the passage over there wouldn't let him disturb me. I've since heard second-hand though, but for you I would have been in a worse pickle."

Aileen smiled wanly and then snuffled, the memory too close and too horrible to control. She dabbed at her eyes with the remnant of a tissue she'd pulled out of her coat.

"I saw the beast hitting you," she said faintly. "He was pitiless, like a demented savage. I didn't even think, I just picked up the baseball bat and swung."

"I'm very glad you did," Lauder said soothingly.

Aileen shook her head as if to jettison the memory, and then looked at him reproachfully. "You tried to cut me out though, didn't you Iain," she said. "That fiction about a visit to Scotland was just designed to keep me away."

Lauder's one good eye momentarily glanced away,

unable to hold her gaze. "I know...I know," he murmured. "I knew it would be violent, and I didn't want you involved."

"I did get involved though, didn't I," Aileen replied with a touch of asperity. "And it's just as well I did."

Lauder wisely retreated into silence. He'd lost the argument on the same issue about a week ago, and was now making a good fist of it again.

"I know why you did it," Aileen said softly, bending forward to give him another kiss. "But I'm not some bimbo who needs a sanitised life, I'm adult enough to take the rough with the smooth, and moreover want it that way, wherever you're concerned."

The room door suddenly opened and a nurse bustled in. In the time it took the woman to reach the bed she conveyed her appreciation of the flowers, how busy it was on the ward and how it wouldn't be wise to overtire Mr Lauder.

"I'd best be going," Aileen said, smiling at him as the nurse pulled and patted at invisible creases in the counterpane.

"Can you give us a little longer, nurse?" Lauder asked.

"A couple of minutes then, Mr Lauder," the woman replied, "but please no longer, I've got to check your pulse, temperature and a few other things."

"What is it, Iain?" Aileen said as the door closed.

Lauder stroked her hand. "Will you get onto Marcus at the Echo – his number's in my directory – and ask him to come to the house as soon as possible, preferably with a photographer. Show him the damage, tell him the story – lay it on thick. We've got to generate as much adverse publicity for the Hunt as we can wreak from the situation."

Aileen raised a hand to her lips and then gave him a wide smile. "It's wonderful to see you're already beginning to mend, darling," she said. "I'll get onto the television people as well."

*

Fred Kerr sat in the small cell looking moodily at the wall. He knew he was in deep shit; there were no two ways about that. He'd been charged on five counts, and from the look on his solicitor's face the pigs wouldn't have to sweat to make them all stick. That cunt, Young, was really up for it – he was loving every minute. He'd already told him – a big grin on his ugly face – they had enough to put him away for a long time.

Kerr gazed bleakly at the small, barred window set high in the wall, the only source of natural light for the cell. Because of the big plum they had against him - causing grievous bodily harm. It was certain, unless some miracle happened, he'd be looking at a view like that for quite a few years to come. He'd been lucky last winter – over that bit of bother in the night club - not to get a gaol sentence; so they'd be doing him no favours this time.

He'd stated of course, he had acted in self-defence; that some of Lauder's injuries weren't down to him, and that Joe and Henshaw must have put their mark on him too. Anything to dirty the waters! The toffee-nosed solicitor might be able to whip something up out of that when he saw him again tomorrow. But Kerr wasn't hopeful. Young had just laughed in his face at the line, pointing out that the Carter skirt had placed him still hammering Lauder after he'd passed out.

The mental picture of the big sergeant, his red grinning face shoved close to his, was still with him. Kerr's fists clenched and unclenched, reliving his rage as he remembered the man's words.

"You're scum, Kerr – a low life, utter scum. You'd say anything to get yourself off the hook. We've had run-ins with you before, and only managed to half nail you once. But this time it's different. We've got you on so many charges it makes your eyes tired reading them. And, above all, we're into you for GBH!"

"I bloody-well tell you," he raged at him, "Lauder went mad when we got in – it was self-defence."

The sergeant's face stayed close to his, but now no

longer smiling, the eyes hard with anger. "Don't waste my time, Kerr – you're as guilty as hell and you know it. Even now in your present straits you're itching to take a pop at me. I can see it in your eyes, you just can't help yourself. You're not alive, not happy, unless you're smashing something or inflicting pain."

The policeman snorted, his mouth curling up at the corners. "The thing is, Kerr you're not fit to be around decent people," he said, "so you need to be put away. And Mrs Carter's statement puts the lid on it; she's stated that she saw you beating Mr Lauder when he was defenceless... Even animals don't behave like that Kerr."

Kerr groaned audibly. All his life he had done much as he pleased. His mother, a small, timid woman, widowed when he was a babe in arms, hadn't been able to control him once his balls had dropped. He'd ruled the roost at home, and being a big lad for his age ruled it at school, the few times he went, that is. Then it was a run of labouring jobs – building sites, working for the council, a spell in a foundry, none lasting long. He'd end up getting grief and his cards, the word 'attitude' cropping up time and time again as he was slammed for drinking too much or sorting out somebody who was picking on him. Until finally he couldn't get work – the word was out on him – and it turned out brilliantly. He began working for the Hunt to top up his dole money – once, sometimes twice, a week during the season he and his terriers were wanted, and it led to the black economy. He found he had more money than when he was employed. If a farmer wanted potatoes lifting, a wall building, he was the man. If an accountant wanted his garden tidying he knew Fred was available. It was cash in hand, and there was never any trouble like before. Kerr watched himself around the members of the Hunt – kept his nature in rein. It didn't do any harm to touch the forelock the odd time, he was fond of telling Golightly, even though they were all wankers.

But some had weighed up just what he was like! For three years ago came all his birthdays rolled into one, a proposition which had put him on easy street. He was making money hand over fist now. He had a bulging building society account, and could even afford to follow England when they went abroad.

It all meant he was freer than ever before. He ran his life just as he wanted without worrying about anyone or anything. If he wanted to get drunk and sleep it off till dinner time the next day, he did it. If he fancied some badgering in the middle of the night, he set off with whoever was game for it. Not for him the chains of marriage; he lived with his dogs in the council house his now dead mother had rented before him, and whenever he wanted a woman he had one. There weren't many in the pubs and clubs of the locality who didn't find his tough, careless attitude interesting; who couldn't be conned into thinking they might be the one to tame Fred!

But now it seemed certain all that was going down the tubes. Young had hinted that with him already having form he could expect eight years. He knew the bastard was trying to put the wind up him. But right or wrong – eight years, five or eighteen months...whatever, it still shook him rigid. Kerr was a man of the open spaces, never happier than when hunting, shooting or fishing. He could only abide four walls for a long time when he was sleeping. He had to have the freedom of being able to move wherever he wanted. Now locked in the small cell with its bed, toilet and washbasin – this was his third day – he was fast reaching screaming point.

He got up from the edge of the bed and began to pace the length of the cell. He had two choices as he saw it. He could say nothing and take the worst they threw at him. Or he could - Kerr swore filthily and hammered the side of his fist into the cell wall - rat to the pigs and have his sentence reduced!

Kerr knew he had next to no scruples. His life was dictated by what he wanted, and he thought only of himself. But the idea of becoming a nark drove him mad. The dust-up in the club last year – a mate had been swinging and butting alongside him. Then when the law arrived Shorty had managed to get out of the bog window. Kerr had taken the medicine, the community sentence and the fine, all of it, and not said a word. He hated informers, anyone who helped the pigs, and had dropped a few in his time. But now he was in this bloody big hole and he just couldn't see a way out.

Young had told him they knew how he made his money, sarcastically pointing out that though he was unemployed he was anything but short. He'd talked about the scruffy but almost new four-by-four Nissan he had, his holidays abroad, and how he was one of the Turk's best customers, if not the best. They'd done their homework on him alright – there were no two ways about that.

"It's not your typical affluent lifestyle," the sergeant sneered, "but it's definitely affluent."

He studied him for a long moment, then said, "You're the main man for this mess, Kerr. If it hasn't dawned yet, the fact that Henshaw and Golightly have been released on bail should clinch it. You're going to be out of it for a long time. That long time could be reduced if you were seen to be helping us. Anyway, think about it." Young said, getting to his feet.

He was thinking about it now. Kerr ceased his pacing and sat down on the bed, He stared at the wall, rubbing a hand through his thick black hair, his brow furrowed. One thing was clear – his days of drug pushing were finished, Driggs would be already busy replacing him. Then once he got out it would be far too dangerous starting again where he left off. Kerr had heard that after you were released the law wasn't too particular about how evidence was got if they knew you were offending again. A burglar he sometimes drank with had told him if they fancied you for a job, you could be having an audience with the Pope and it wouldn't matter. So the message was plain – he had nothing to lose in that way.

Young had said, and repeated it, that it was only information they wanted. There'd be no statement required, no chance of being used in the future to testify – no-one outside the force would know. He'd also said he wouldn't be incriminating himself; that they needed evidence of possession or drugs being passed which, he knew, they wouldn't now be getting. All they wanted, the man insisted, the pig of a face again close to his, was pointing in the right direction, how the stuff came into the country and the name or names of the people involved.

Kerr allowed himself a cheerless smile. It was certainly rich that Young had interviewed Driggs last week over the Lauder business. The lump of shite wouldn't have the slightest idea that the man whose fireside he sat in front of was Mr Big, the prime mover who had most of the Northumbrian CID regularly leaping about.

He didn't know how Driggs got the stuff on the continent, of course. He didn't know much; after being told a few times to mind his own bloody business and concentrate on what he, Driggs, wanted, he'd kept his mouth shut. All he did know was that the man about every six weeks left Newcastle Airport in his Cessna for a two or three day trip to Holland; somewhere near Rotterdam, he thought. As to how he got the stuff over there, Kerr had no idea. But it wouldn't be hard. Amsterdam for instance – he'd been there with England a few years ago – was a pot smoker's heaven. Cannabis was on sale in nearly every coffee shop in the city, and with it being a big port as well he would bet the harder stuff like cocaine was available in plenty. Then it was back to Newcastle at night, and that was the classy bit. Driggs would turf the container out over his own land and then go on to land at the airport.

Kerr had to hand it to the man. Driggs was a real wanker, but he ran a business which was as sweet as a nut. He'd put him in clover to the extent that he could now stump up the forty grand his part of the action cost in one go. As to how many others like him were involved, Kerr could only guess. All he knew was that on his visits to the farm the time he spent there was rationed. Small talk was out. Driggs would say what he wanted, hand over the stuff, take the money and show him the door. It was like an army operation, and usually there would be the headlights of another vehicle turning onto the drive as he was leaving.

He gazed morosely at the wall. He would have a hard time finding another earner anything like it when he got out. With his team of four – all unemployed, whom he ruled with the rod of iron – he'd covered the area from Corbridge to the head of the Tyne valley. The demand was getting bigger all the time, and it wasn't just kids either. The snotty-nosed brigade was at it too – recreational ingestion they called it. He now had a band of customers not only in his own Hunt, but in neighbouring ones too. And on top of that it was easy work – only occupying him a couple of days a week. There were places, going west towards the Pennines, where they couldn't get enough of it; where he could clear ten thousand in a few hours. So all in all he was going to have a bugger of a job to even begin matching that sort of return.

But there was a way. It would take time once he got out, but he had the money to get started. He could have a stab at the import business. More and more, the Coalition, and Labour before them, were making fags and spirits a big earner if you could get the stuff across the water. He knew a lad down at North Shields who was doing just that. He'd got sick of the quotas, hadn't wetted the boat's nets for two years and was coining it. Tom had said a few times he could do with him – to help with the landings to move bulk. And another thing was sure: the law wasn't bothered about booze and fags the way they were about drugs. They knew about the trade which went on in the pubs and clubs but rarely lifted a finger.

Kerr stood up, deciding. It wasn't as if Driggs was a mate, he thought, as he crossed the cell to press the buzzer. But he wanted firm promises before he opened his mouth, and he didn't trust Young. He would tell him Inspector Moran had to be there, and it wouldn't be a bad idea if his solicitor was around too. He thumbed the bell, gave an itch near his groin a satisfying scratch and then lit a cigarette.

CHAPTER ELEVEN

Driggs pushed the papers on his desk to one side, his expression severe. He was in no mood to assess stock prices, which was hardly surprising. The weekend news had gradually filtered out and all of it was grave. Filtered was the right word, because most of it had come from Golightly. The man had rather reluctantly, it seemed, been pressed into giving an account of the incident. That prime idiot, Henshaw couldn't be contacted; he'd holed up at home and was refusing to answer either the door or the telephone. Achilles sulking in his tent was a loose analogy, except it was a dire insult to the Greek's memory.

If he had been told of the composition of the visiting party beforehand he would have said it was a recipe for disaster. Mix Kerr, wild and pugnacious, needing strong control, with a hate driven Henshaw and you immediately had the ingredients for a massive foul up. What should have been a frightening or a bloody nose at the most had developed into a brutal civil war. They'd made Lauder almost a martyr. And now the Hunt was in the process of being crucified for it. He had to discard the morning paper an hour ago, so vitriolic was the language being used.

That woman Dodds – now acting Master, God help them all – had just been on the phone practically wetting himself; saying the resignations and excuses had started to flood in. Apparently even Alec Ritson, a long time stalwart, had said he would no longer be riding with them. He didn't like the man, but it was a big blow and served to pave the way for the waverers and doubters. He knew these things acquired a momentum of their own, became self-escalating. And Dodds was the last man to deal with it. You needed a cool head to steady the ship, someone to assure everyone the gale would eventually moderate. Instead they had this wimp bleating like a castrated tup, which was no damned good and he'd told him so.

But for Driggs there was an even larger problem

attached to the big one. It was Kerr. The word was, according to the morning paper, he was seen as the worst transgressor. He'd been denied bail because he'd been accused of GBH in addition to other charges. A thin worm of alarm began to writhe at the back of Driggs' mind. He got up and moved to look out of the study window. He'd been in tight corners before, he told himself. That landing last winter in the Cessna, for instance – the fog had been so bad you couldn't tell where it ended and the ground started. The trick was not to get emotional but to continue thinking.

There were two possible scenarios, he reckoned, composing himself. Kerr could remain schtum; after all, what they had him for wasn't drugs related. He would want to protect their relationship, reasoning he could resume his role once released. Or the man would trade information, namely throw him to the dogs, in return for a less severe sentence.

Driggs wasn't at all inclined to the first: Kerr, besides having the survival instincts of a rat, wasn't a fool. He would have realised that as soon as he was convicted he'd be a marked man on his release to society, and therefore the man would know – he knew him well enough – that from his standpoint he became unemployable the minute he was arrested.

So there it was, stark and thoroughly frightening but, nevertheless, it had to be confronted. The second scenario was the realistic one. He was no longer any use to Kerr; so, if it hadn't already happened, his name would be a pawn in some tawdry accommodation between the thug and the police.

Driggs had known it would come to this one day. You couldn't work with toe-rags indefinitely without eventually suffering repercussions. The unwashed and the limited were the weak link in what was otherwise a superb business. A business which he now had to accept was in its death throes. He realised he couldn't revamp the operation. It wasn't as if he was some cryptic figure pulling strings in the background. He was the planner, financier, carrier and distributor all merged into one. He preferred it that way – the profits were even larger and he had direct control over every aspect of the process. But now he would be receiving CID's undivided attention. There would be no dawn raids on his house, nothing dramatic like that. The rat, Kerr, had doubtless told them he was meticulous in disposing of the stuff, that he couldn't tolerate it in his home for more than a few hours. So they'd be watching and enquiring, waiting for him to pull his flying boots on.

Still, he'd had a marvellous run. The seven figure sum in the Swiss bank, plus the fine things he'd accumulated, testified to that. The pity was, another trip and he would have had the cash to replace the Cessna outright. And there was also the galling matter of the banker's draft he'd sent his supplier just five days ago. Driggs gazed bleakly out of the shut window. That hurt; it was for £100,000, non-refundable, and the advance payment for another consignment...

*

Lauder sipped from the coffee cup and then rather deliberately put it on the table in front of him. The steady drone of a vacuum cleaner came from the room next door. Aileen had moved in on his return from hospital. She'd taken leave from work and now a week later he didn't have the slightest idea what he would have done without her.

He winced as he reached for the coffee again. Although his other injuries were well on their way to mending, his ribs were still troublesome. The doctors had told him that, inevitably, it must be a slow process. The very act of breathing – they had explained – with the constant expansion and contraction of the chest, meant the re-knitting of the bones took longer than in most other locations of the body. Then there was the itching. Sometimes he thought that worse than the continual dull ache. The inability to get behind the tight strapping and deal with the offending spot, threatened at times to drive him frantic. He was really looking forward to tomorrow when the district nurse was due to call in order to change his bandages. The doughty woman was now synonymous with deliverance in his mind, her twice-weekly visits coinciding with the twin luxuries of a splendid scratch and then a thorough shower before he was encased again.

But there were other visitors expected, and very shortly. In fact in twenty minutes, Lauder thought, glancing at his watch. A television team, responsible for weekly, in-depth broadcast on topical matters, was coming. Their objectives were to cover the night of terror, as the producer had so dramatically described it on the phone a couple of days ago, and then to make the case that in the light of the Hunt's involvement, the pending Bill to legitimise hunting must be completely shelved. Lauder was quite content with that approach. The man was clearly an avowed 'anti', and rather than making bullets he would be fashioning shells, and firing them with great gusto to boot.

And that had been much the pattern since his discharge from hospital. Apart from a few photographs, events had progressed without there being a great deal of input required from him. He had to thank Aileen for that. As the sound of the hoover got nearer, indicating preparations were well advanced for the arrival of the TV crew, he had reason to reflect on the emergence of a considerable talent: the facility with which she could manage public relations.

She'd been a revelation, still was, and it began the Monday after his admission to hospital. Marcus, she later told him, besides being evidently concerned for his welfare, had an air of professional excitement about him within seconds of entering the house. Barbarians, scum, septic bastards, were some of the epithets used as he directed the young photographer and saw the extent of the damage.

"My God, Aileen," he cried at one point. "What they

must have put Iain through!"

Then it was a dash to the hospital, where Aileen inveigled a short interview from the Consultant. They all had to suppress smiles as the man declared, "But for Mr Lauder's continued improvement and the fact it was high-time stumps were finally drawn on fox hunting," he wouldn't be acceding to such an invasion.

The Echo burst the story onto the public the following morning. It was given front page coverage, with a photograph of himself in his mummified condition, others of the havoc within the house. The one-inch high headline demanded, "What did this man do to the Hunt to deserve such bestiality?"

Aileen was then off. Having given Marcus his exclusive she agreed to further conducted tours for national newspapers, their interest turbo-charged because of the Echo's disclosures. Then it was the turn of the regional TV to be shown the wreckage. Repairs had to wait, even those to the dining room window and the front door, which caused the insurers some disquiet for a couple of days. While there was a camera around to be trained, either from the press or TV, Aileen gave them a free hand.

By the end of the first week, when he was on the brink of being released from hospital, he found he had a well-established media officer. If the attention of the news-mongers showed signs of flagging Aileen would nudge them back into overdrive. Her tactics widened to embrace politicians. She flew to London, and via Heathrow arrived at the Houses of Parliament for a much publicised meeting with a coterie of anti-hunting MPs. Then it was into one of the national TV studios for an acrimonious clash with Davidson, the Conservative MP for their constituency.

The man almost immediately got off on the wrong foot, grandly pronouncing the matter sub judice and therefore the guilt of those charged not proven. To which Aileen tartly replied she didn't give a fig for his Latin expressions, and was he not overlooking the fact she'd been there? Was it a figment of her imagination that the

Hunt Master was hooded like an Al Qaeda terrorist? Or had she dreamt that she happened on the Hunt's terrier man half killing her fiancé? Davidson visibly deflated like a punctured balloon and never recovered, stumbling and blustering his way to the end of the exchange.

It was all bread, butter and jam for the media. It seemed to Lauder he couldn't turn on the TV or pick up a newspaper without his picture, or Aileen's, or both, being prominently displayed. And throughout the Hunt floundered, grew increasingly enfeebled, as the tide of the adverse publicity battered them. The new Master, Dodds, making his debut on the regional news a few nights before, typified the condition. When pointedly asked why some of his members had invaded Mr Lauder's home and savagely beaten him, he procrastinated and evaded. Then when pressed by the interviewer, Dodds lost his temper and, placing himself in an even worse light, ludicrously attacked the young woman for misrepresenting events.

Lauder could understand the man's invidious position. The Hunt, throughout his clandestine campaign against them, had never publicly acknowledged any harassment. Apart from the incident at Driggs' farm there'd been no complaints to the police, no statements of outrage to the media. So much so that at times he thought himself operating in a vacuum. It was simply, of course, that the Hunt didn't wish to admit they were the subject of such activities; to do so would inevitably mean much unwanted attention. Nor could they use the episode at the Driggs' place – the laws of slander wouldn't permit it. He'd had his car stolen that night; was at home when Mr Driggs had been treated so roughly. The police had subsequently recovered the vehicle, and the official explanation was that persons unknown were responsible for the theft. Accordingly, not one of them could publicly so much as hint at his involvement. Apart from the legal implications it would be seen as yet another example of the Hunt's scurrilous behaviour.

So the hapless Dodds was required to defend the

indefensible, clearly a task beyond even a much more intelligent character. For the public perception, fuelled by the constant media coverage, was wholly sympathetic, namely, that he, Lauder had been brutally beaten and his home wrecked because he'd spoken out about how wrong it was to scrap the hunting ban.

It spanked of the thought police in some totalitarian state, conjured images of red coats substituted for the Nazi brown shirts of the Third Reich. The story was sensational and damning, and as much as the Hunt would prefer, refused to die.

And now it was spawning other dramatic news. Yesterday morning's Echo had featured an article on the ex-Hunt Master, Henshaw. Apparently his shops were being boycotted, so, on police bail and awaiting trial, the man was also facing early financial ruin. A photograph accompanied the report, showing a rather desolate figure in a striped apron standing outside empty premises, and as one of the shop windows was cracked in two places, it was plain the public's antipathy wasn't entirely passive.

Then, hardly had it been able to absorb that, the Hunt received another colossal blow. Last night's national TV news highlighted an item which would previously have been unthinkable: the sight of the Conservative politician for a shire constituency, their MP Davidson, on his feet in the Commons doing a volte-face. Perhaps Aileen's scathing words to him of a few days before had triggered the transformation. But whatever the reason there he was to be seen, peering round the chamber over drooping spectacles, condemning the actions and complicity of the leading members of the local Hunt. He said that while he was aware that due legal process had yet to run its course he could no longer support those involved. Then, to some peptic expressions on the front bench, he widened his comments, saying that the whole episode had caused him to re-examine long held beliefs, and he was now of the opinion that hunting with dogs was an anachronism and therefore didn't have a place in Britain's civilised society.

Lauder remembered Aileen's flabbergasted peal of delight. "Oh my!" she cried, eyes sparkling. "Old weathervane, Davidson has done it again. Would I love to be a fly on his surgery wall this weekend!"

Her elation was understandable. It was a huge propaganda coup, probably the biggest to date. Here was one of the old guard of reactionary Tory MPs repudiating a movement he'd championed all his political life. He was the arch filibuster when it came to anti-hunting legislation. The man who'd consigned the first private member's bill of the nineties to the scrap heap by reading interminably to the House from a London telephone directory. That he was prepared to ditch his former allies so summarily showed how strongly the pendulum of public opinion was moving against them.

Altogether things were going tremendously well, Lauder mused. They had achieved far more than he dared hope that day when, knowing he was uncovered, he decided to somehow manipulate the aggression he was facing. The incident had physically cost him a lot but, perversely, was the stuff of the success they were enjoying. Had Henshaw and his unholy crew quit once they realised he was going to resist them; contented themselves with the damage and fright they'd already caused, it would have been just another frustrated attempt at burglary, barely meriting a few lines in the local paper. But he had correctly gauged the mentality of his visitors, and they'd played wholly into his hands. Although, he wryly thought, his fingers touching the collar supporting his jaw, the outcome wasn't quite what he'd intended.

The lounge door was pushed open. "Iain," Aileen said quietly, rather gingerly holding up a small revolver, "what's this I've just found in one of the bedroom drawers?"

"That," replied Lauder, more evenly than he felt, taking the gun from her, "is a memento from the Allies' campaign in northern Europe and left to me by my father along with his fob-watch and a few other things."

"Oh, I thought...." she exclaimed, and, clearly flustered, tailed off.

"Don't worry, it's never been fired, and nor will it ever be." He stroked the stock which bore the inscription 'M & R Arms Co, Massachusetts'. "I think the old man was given it by an American G I."

Aileen suddenly looked at him appraisingly, "I thought you were going to wear your new pullover," she said. "The TV people will be here any minute, and you can't be interviewed in that thing you've got on."

Lauder grinned at her. She was the picture of domestic femininity, clad in an apron with a lock of fair hair falling across her lovely face. "I was just about to do it," he said untruthfully, as he levered himself rather mechanically out of the chair.

She helped him into the garment. Then she was quickly discarding the apron and smoothing down her dress as the sound of a vehicle arriving reached their ears. "I'll let them in," she called over her shoulder, heading for the hall. "But remember what we agreed – greet them in the kitchen right below the damaged ceiling."

Lauder smiled again. He felt almost sorry for the Hunt, the vast majority of whom would have had no knowledge of what Henshaw intended. But now lumped together with the Neanderthal and his odious henchmen, they were shortly to be battered by another tidal wave of atrocious publicity.

*

Sergeant Young received a cup of tea from the Detective Constable beside him and grunted his appreciation. Yates, an indistinct figure in the darkness of the car, screwed the cap back on the thermos flask, then picked up his cup.

It was fifteen minutes to midnight. The two of them were sat in an unmarked vehicle in the lay-by on the military road, bordering the Driggs' farm. Outside the weather was cold; a keen north-west wind was sending the temperature lower and lower, and there would be a frost before daylight broke.

Yates watched one of the few vehicles now using the road to go past, then turned to Young. "He sounds a prime villain, this Driggs, sergeant," the young man observed.

"He is, lad," Young replied. "Not that you'd notice on meeting him. He's every inch the gentleman farmer – collected, rides with the hounds and all that, besides being a fearless flyer."

"If he offloads a few pounds of dope from his plane tonight, we'll have the bugger," Yates said, an edge of excitement to his voice. "And what a collar that will be."

"It will...; but best not count our chickens, aye."

Young looked meditatively across the fields to the black shape of Driggs' farmhouse. They'd learned from the airport authorities that their bird had taken wing last Sunday, three days ago. Apparently his destination was somewhere in Holland, a place near Rotterdam, he thought, although he wasn't sure. Then another call had come in early evening to say Driggs was on his way back. He'd filed a flight plan and the word was he was due to land at Newcastle about twenty minutes after twelve, just before operations ceased for the night.

The radio crackled into life, and an instantly recognisable voice with a soft Scottish accent came on the air. It was Chief Inspector Moran parked in a second car, roughly five miles to the west of them.

"Just checking that the damn thing's working, George. We don't want to be caught dumb when Biggles puts in an appearance."

Young picked up the handset. "I can hear you fine, Bill," he said. "In fact you woke us both up." There were chuckles at the far end, a brief acknowledgement, then the line went dead.

"Funny how the business with Lauder kicked all this off," Yates said deferentially, clearly impressed with the easy familiarity Young had just displayed towards his boss.

Young nodded. "You're right there. He started the chain of events that put us here tonight."

"He's making rings around the Hunt," Yates said. "I saw him interviewed on the TV the other night, and apart from some lip he gave them at times, he couldn't explain why they treated him so savagely. Their spokesman was stuttering and stammering throughout."

"Wouldn't explain, more like," Young asserted. "He's done plenty - he belted Driggs for a kick-off. We weren't able to prove it because he covered himself, but he did. Driggs shoved a shotgun into his woman's face so Lauder floored him." He looked reflectively at the Detective Constable for a moment. "The quiet word is he's been running around in the middle of the night upsetting them something rotten – pinning insulting notices to their kitchen windows and that sort of thing."

"But there's never been any complaints of trespass or intimidation," Yates replied. "Nothing like that."

"Exactly," Young said, "that's the point. Publicly they've treated him like a non-person, as if he didn't exist. They didn't want to admit that somebody was so pissed off with their activities he was prepared to go to those lengths. I doubt if we would have even heard about the incident with Driggs if his wife hadn't panicked and phoned us."

"Particularly since he, most of all," Yates observed, "would want to keep a low profile – not draw attention to himself."

Young nodded and glanced sideways at the young man. "So the Hunt ends up in a wringer," he said. "Three of their members – and there must have been pre-knowledge on the part of a few others – beat the shit out of Lauder, half-killed him. And they can't even begin to justify what happened. To belly-ache about him now, apart from being actionable, would be seen as trying to harm somebody they'd already abused. They're in a hell of a fix – couldn't have put themselves in a worse position."

"Suits me," Yates said with a force which surprised Young. "I've always thought they were a bunch of bastards anyway."

Young grinned at him in the darkness of the car's interior. "Now then, lad," he said half mockingly, "we can't allow our personal feelings to surface, we've got to stay impartial."

Yates' head swung round to regard him. "I'll act impartially, sergeant," he said quietly, "no matter how I feel."

The radio suddenly burst into life with the sound of Moran's voice. "A twin-engine plane's coming in from the south-west, George," the man said. "It's fairly low and seems to be heading for Newcastle, so it's got to be him."

"Ok, Bill," Young answered, "we're ready over here. We'll see you soon."

"Right, detective," Young murmured, replacing the hand set with one hand and removing some binoculars from the compartment in front of him with the other. "Let's find out what Mr Driggs is posting tonight."

He got out of the car and walked about ten yards to a point which gave him an unobstructed view to the south. It was a clear, starry night and he could see all the lights of the river towns, Prudhoe, Crawcrook, Blaydon, tracing the path of the Tyne down to the huge sprawl of Newcastle and its suburbs. As Yates hurried to his side he cast a sideways glance at the vehicle, tucked in next to the hedge and under the canopies of two large firs for good measure, he was sure the black Ford couldn't be detected from the air. He turned and began to train the glasses on the night sky to the south-west.

"There it is!" Yates exclaimed, the younger and keener eyes delivering first.

Young swung his glasses fractionally, following the pointing arm of the Detective Constable. "But it's too far away," he cried as the winking red and green navigation lights came into sight. "It's not going to pass anywhere near here."

He continued to watch the aeroplane, his heart sinking. It was about four miles due south of them, flying in a west to east direction along the course of the river. The aircraft would shortly turn north and begin its descent to the airport. There would certainly be no post that night!

The throb of engines dwindled, and Young lowered his binoculars to glance at the crestfallen Yates. "No result tonight, lad..." he started to say, when another black Ford veered off the road and crunched to a halt beside them. Moran and Gore emerged, their postures and expressions immediately conveying they knew too.

"Aye, I half-expected this George," the bulky figure of Moran said. He leaned forward, cradling his hands against the breeze to light a cigarette. "Nothing's ever easy in this job."

"It seems as if we've lost our chance, Bill," Young said flatly.

"I don't know George," Moran replied, exhaling a cloud of smoke. "Could be more a case of chappie not working to our script."

"What next then, sir?" Yates enquired.

"I'm afraid, son, for you it's here until the end of the shift. Well, not here but tucked up that cart track in the woods half a mile back. Chappie obviously knows we're onto him, so I think you'll find he'll come home and go straight to bed."

He glanced at Gore. "Give him that extra flask of tea, Constable – it's unopened so should still be hot."

Young smiled to himself and shook his head. He'd never met a Chief Inspector who was a patch on Bill Moran. If he needed more confirmation of his qualities here was another example. That act of consideration, in the immediate aftermath of what he realised was a sizeable setback, was the stock in trade of a decent intelligent man. Yates wouldn't doze through a long, difficult stint in the coming hours – he would stay alert, want to make a contribution. He had his sense of duty and above all he wouldn't want to let the Jock down, as Moran was affectionately known throughout the station.

"And it's back to the luxuries of the nick for us,

George," Moran said. He turned, pulling his dark overcoat closer around him, and headed for the nearest car.

*

Forty-five minutes later Young walked down an empty corridor leading to Moran's office. The station was quiet, as was usually the case most week nights in the early hours. He'd assigned Gore to a burglary enquiry along with another officer, so he plus Moran and the desk officer were the only staff on the premises.

He knocked on the door and went in. Moran glanced up from the map he was poring over and waved him to the chair facing his desk.

"Help yourself, George – keeps the chill out and life worth living," he said, sliding a bottle of Glenlivet across the desk surface towards him. Young smiled, selected a tumbler from the row on top of a nearby filing cabinet, poured himself a measure and sat down. He looked at the Chief Inspector expectantly, knowing as much as it might seem otherwise he was in for another brain-storming session.

Moran swung his legs to one side of the desk and sat back in the chair. "I'm getting fat," he complained, drawing a hand across his ample stomach. "Ella's cooking, cars, driving this bloody desk, the booze... it's unstoppable. I tell you in another few years I'll need a block and tackle to get out of this chair."

Young looked warmly at the man. The face reminded him of a boxer dog – heavy jowls, flat nose and lively eyes, all surmounted by a mop of sandy hair. "It's nearly everybody's problem nowadays, Bill," he remarked.

"Aye..., but it's no consolation," Moran growled. "Anyway, George, any thoughts on tonight... you've met this Driggs haven't you?"

Young drank and then nursed the whiskey in his big hands. "The thing I keep coming back to is why did he make the trip? He's not stupid – he's realised that low life

Kerr must have talked," he paused, eyeing Moran. "And it's the same conclusion every time, he's put money out front."

The pleasant but ugly face grinned at him. "Snap... that's exactly what I thought too," Moran said. "So where is the stuff?"

Young shrugged. "You've got me there, Bill," he said, "somewhere in the Netherlands I expect, under lock and key."

"There's another possibility, look at this." Moran stood up and twisted a portion of an ordnance survey map through ninety degrees. Some of his papers slid off the desk but went unheeded. "Do you see the line I've drawn?" he said, pointing. "Well, that's the direction he came from as best as I can estimate it. I've asked for a copy of the flight plan but that's close enough."

Young studied the map. It was for an area below a line between Corbridge and Haltwhistle, the route of the trunk road, the A69. He saw the contour lines narrow as the rich farming land of the Tyne valley changed to upland terrain in the south.

"I watched chappie come up from there," Moran murmured, following his eyes. "That's wild inhospitable country, George."

"You think he did his posting somewhere down there?" Young said incredulously.

"What better... what better?" Moran replied, his eyes gleaming. "If chappie can't drop on his own land, knee high heather is the next best thing. No-one can see where the package is lying, there's no chance of a farmer ploughing it under... just the odd sheep having a nose."

"But how would he find it?" Young exclaimed. "He could look for days, and only end up drawing attention to himself."

"Aye, if I'm right and I think I am, that's the clever part," Moran said. "Have you ever heard of these radio bugs, George?"

"Aren't they being used now by some of the city boys

to recover stolen cars?"

"That's right. They're being installed in high specification Mercs, BMWs... beasties like that. They emit a radio beam which can be picked up by a hand held receiver several miles away. It pinpoints position so if the bad boys don't go out of town fast, they're in big trouble."

"And you think Driggs could have put one of these devices in with the drugs?" Young said questioningly.

"Why not... why not?" Moran urged. "If you accept the original premise that he'd paid for the stuff in advance, then it all flows from there. Chappie is greedy, has nerve and above all – listening to all I've heard about him lately – thinks himself a cut above. He didn't go to Holland to put stuff in a left-luggage locker, a safe or whatever. He's sure he can outsmart a bunch of flat feet like us... thinks if he doesn't do a drop where we expected, we'll go away wringing our hands."

"By God, Bill... it makes sense," Young cried, beginning to catch some of Moran's enthusiasm. "So we watch him like a hawk in the days ahead."

"We'll keep an eye out of course," Moran said thoughtfully, "but I don't want to deter him. I was thinking more of concentrating our resources at the other end."

Young grinned at him. "I know now why I'm sitting at this side of the desk and you're over there... You'll have to explain that one."

"Put yourself in Driggs' shoes, George," Moran demanded, leaning across the desk towards him. "You're at a thousand feet, coming up the Pennines... Apart from rough ground what are your other requirements for posting the stuff?"

Young amassed his thoughts. "I'd want," he said, starting slowly, "to drop in an area I knew fairly well. Then I'd want to drop near a quiet road, the lonelier the better. And thirdly I'd need some sort of landmark to give me an approximate fix on where I should later begin looking. That last is the snag: it's moorland, no distinguishing marks at all."

"Not quite, George... thanks to a cataclysmic event which happened millions of years ago."

Young smiled and spread his big frame more easily in the chair. The chief inspector was off and about to expand on his all consuming hobby – geology. He knew the man was never happier than when examining stream beds, eroded hillsides, the spoil heaps of disused mines. Young had seen his extensive collection of mineral samples, and the beauty of some of the specimens, their crystalline facets glinting in the garden sunlight like so many precious stones, was a memory he would not easily forget.

"An underground volcanic mass which pushed up, forming the North Pennines," Moran went on, "and provided valuable minerals that man has been working since Roman times."

"You're talking about mining and metal extraction."

"Exactly," Moran burst out, a couple of flecks of spittle descending onto the desktop. He brandished a dog-eared envelope, pointing at the back. "Look what I wrote down two minutes before you came into the room – rough ground, not too far from Hexham, lonely road and a tall chimney!"

Young glanced at the notes, glad the scrawl had been read out to him. "What chimney?" he asked, mystified.

"That chimney," Moran said, stabbing his finger at the ordnance survey map. "It was the stack for a lead-smelting furnace in the nineteenth century, and is one of the few still standing as far as I can recollect... That's your landmark. It's right under chappie's flight path and the only relief in mile upon mile of featureless moor."

Young craned forward to examine the map. He felt another twinge of excitement as he realised the direction of Moran's bold red line met all the requirements they'd attributed to Driggs. The terrain was difficult; the landmark was there; it crossed one of the least used roads he knew, the route from Blanchland via the moors to Waskerley, and was perhaps a thirty minute drive from the Tyne valley.

Moran grinned at him. "There's even a 'des-res' for Gore and Brean," he said, pointing at a location on the map marked 'ruin' and about a couple of hundred yards away from the chimney.

"They'll need some of your Glenlivet, Bill, if they hole up in there for any length of time," Young chuckled.

The Scot's smile suddenly faded. "I'm going to throw everything I have at this, George," he said grimly. "If Driggs brought the stuff in, and I'm sure he did, then what we've outlined happened. He's a wee man making pounds ten off the back of misery and weakness, and it's high time he was put away."

"I'll drink to that," Young said, raising the glass to his lips.

CHAPTER TWELVE

Driggs stood at the bedroom window with his binoculars, looking over the fields to the military road. He fixed on a spot for a moment, moved the glasses fractionally to either side and then lowered them. He remained looking in the same direction, a thoughtful expression on his hawk-like features. The cart track at the far side of the road was again empty. That hadn't been the case the day after he returned, nor the following. But the black Ford hadn't been evident since.

He was inclined to think the police had decided there wasn't much they could do for the time being. He realised they needed to catch him in possession; wouldn't make a move unless that was probable. And since he hadn't accommodated them last week and they knew he didn't keep the stuff on the premises, it seemed they had turned to more pressing matters.

Certainly the events of the last eight days bore out the analysis. He'd been out three times since his return, and on none of those occasions had he thought himself followed or anyone evincing more than a normal interest in him. The first had been a gathering organised by his wine club in Newcastle; the second, and what a poor affair that had been — quarter of the usual turnout and bloody protestors howling from every thicket — the weekly meet. Then a couple of nights ago he'd met an old school chum, a fellow art-collector, in a hotel up the North Tyne valley. It was an out of the way place, deliberately chosen by him, but again nothing had happened to arouse his suspicions. Apart from a couple of hill farmers — their conversation peppered with reference to mart prices and the bastard government — no-one else followed him into the small cocktail bar.

The reality appeared to be that the police had mounted an operation on the basis of Kerr's singing, failed to entrap him and then stood down. There was probably a report already on the Chief Constable's desk saying they'd severely curtailed the activities of a substantial drug business, had one of the principal pushers in custody, and were now awaiting further development in importation.

But then was he being encouraged to think along those lines? Driggs asked himself, his face hardening. Could it be that the police strategy was designed to lull him into a false sense of security? Might the 'plods' have exercised some grey matter for once and reasoned he had brought the drugs in but fooled them over the drop zone! It could be that from the cover of the woods the house and he were being watched continually, that tailing was highly selective – abandoned as soon as it was established he was acting ordinarily., the whole thrust of the plan to make him think it safe to commit himself.

Driggs snorted, this was surely the path to paranoia. Whatever the police were or weren't up to, he roughly told himself, made no difference. He had laid his plans and there was no chance of anyone staying in contact with him tonight.

He dropped a small Adidas bag onto the bed and began packing. First a pair of sturdy walking boots, then shaving gear, pyjamas and a change of underwear. That would serve him for the overnight stay in the hotel on the A68 near Castleford. There was no need for anything more. The clothes he wore – yellow patterned cravat, dark brown sweater and tailored beige pants – were quite suitable for a hotel dining room midweek. He would see the infamous five – previously six – individually for the last time in the privacy of his own room. Then a pleasant celebratory dinner with probably a bottle of Moet and Chandon to mark the occasion. He zipped up the carrying bag, lifted it from the bed and went downstairs.

Half an hour later Vera did as he instructed and pulled the Land Rover to a halt. She'd stopped just past the intersection of Hallgate bank and the main road on the periphery of Hexham town centre. Driggs received a peck on the cheek and quickly swung his legs from the vehicle to hurry up the one-way system. He got almost to the top of the steep hill before looking back. An old woman, head bent towards the descending traffic as she toiled upwards was the only occupant of the footpath behind him.

That was fine, he thought, beginning to merge with the crowds in the market place, the magnificence of the Abbey to his right. If the mounted brigade were following, and he must work on that assumption, they would be temporarily disadvantaged. The danger now lay in an officer patrolling the vicinity on foot hearing by radio of his presence.

Driggs chose one of the cobbled side streets rather than the wide, pedestrian walkway to reach the far side of the town. He kept his eyes skinned, moving along behind a throng of shoppers; once stopping in a dimly lit doorway to covertly watch the people approaching.

But no-one gave him more than a brief glance and he saw nothing untoward. A patrol car passed as he stood in the melee at the lights waiting to cross the high street. Then he was at the other side and hurrying round a corner to enter the garage premises.

The owner was patently pleased to see him. While unsaid, at ten to six in the late afternoon with close of business near and darkness descending, all the signs were it had been a slow day for car hire. He was shown what appeared to be the firm's entire stock and chose a dark green Mondeo. Twenty minutes later, having paid for a day's hire and completed the appropriate forms he nosed his way into the traffic.

Driggs felt the first stirrings of elation as he motored east out of the town; so far, so very good he thought. He'd effectively detached himself from the identification tag of the Land Rover and seemingly in the process slipped the law. Unless he'd been spotted entering the car hire premises, or the police, guessing his intentions, had moved swiftly to contact the two outlets in Hexham – both unlikely eventualities – he was all but beyond their grasp. Nevertheless while a risk remained, however slight, he was going to make damned sure he stayed careful.

On the outskirts of Riding Mill before the long, straight stretch to the junction of the A68, he acted again. With two cars coming up behind him he took the blind bend emerging from the village then executed a sharp left to end up parked, engine and lights doused, on a row of residential houses. Neither of the vehicles faltered, and through a gap between two bungalows he could see their headlights streaming towards the roundabout in the distance. He waited a couple of minutes but no car crawled back through the village examining the side roads. Nor, when he did eventually reach the roundabout to turn south on the A68, was there any sign of vehicles parked or acting suspiciously.

He repeated the routine a quarter of an hour later. He drove onto the premises of the inn, just before the Blanchland turnoff, and found a space between two cars. There were about fifteen vehicles drawn up outside the old coaching house; he'd enjoyed a meal there before and clearly it was still popular. He sat for about ten minutes, the awesome black expanse of the moors stretching away to the south and west of him. Then, timing his re-entry to coincide with a lull in the sparse traffic, he fleetingly joined the main road before turning for Blanchland.

Driggs brought the Ford to a halt and, slapping the dashboard with the palm of his hand, erupted with delight. He was home and dry! Whatever pursuit there'd been he had left floundering – it would be plain sailing from now on! He picked the receiver up from the passenger seat, flicked the on-button and directed it at the dim outline of the single track road rising in front of him. A red dot appeared on the dial, beeping insistently, slightly to the left of the line he was pointing in. His treasure trove awaited him! Unless, of course, he chortled there was somebody in that tumble-down building up there, already in touch with several police cars secreted around the area. He burst out laughing again, the receiver slipping through his fingers to fall on his lap.

A huge feeling, a mixture of elation and relief, swept over Gore as he watched the indistinct figure of Driggs coming up the bridle path. A rare shaft of moonlight penetrating the thick low cloud overhead had identified him about thirty seconds ago; which was just as well since neither he nor Brean recognised the car, lights dowsed and parked below them at the beginning of the track, as one of those the farmer owned

From near the gaping hole which had once constituted the other window in the crumbling bothy the shadowy form of his older colleague whispered, "He's a clever bugger is our Driggs, that," motioning his head towards the stationary vehicle, a smudge in the distance "must be a hire car."

"Tell me about it, Reggie." Gore replied, the pleasant open face settling into a frown. "He's not only careful but hyper-careful. I should know the bastard's been on top of my life for the last ten days"

He looked after the retreating figure now almost obscured by the gloom, the man's bearing only revealed by a series of tiny, blood-red pulses from the transponder he held. He saw the signals suddenly veer to the right, towards the edge of the path as he acknowledged to himself that rather than acting like a dispassionate professional he'd allowed Driggs to really get under his skin. First two nights of cold lonely observation, cooped up in an unmarked car, opposite but well away from the scum-bag's large, prosperous-looking farm Then four or five days when he had been able to return to something like normal life with his fiancée; marred, as she pointedly told him one night, because the man was so patently preoccupying his thoughts. In short the period when they were luring him out, springing the trap as the Chief had put it. Now three nights of intensely cold awful surveillance, the bothy cruelly draughty, a toilet for every sheep in the neighbourhood, the stone flagged floor covered with old and fresh- the worst smelling-droppings. This was their third night of sufferance, the memories of which now rapidly fading because the 'jock' had once again got it spot-on!

As Brean thumbed numbers on the station-issued mobile and then spoke quietly into the mouthpiece, Gore glanced backwards at the two rug-sacks in the most sheltered part of the building. It was the corner farthest away from the area where the rotten roof timbers had finally succumbed to the weight of the slates, leaving a ragged gap about a fifth of the bothy's dimensions in size. Last night had been the worst – heavy icy rain for about two hours and the strong wind slanting it in so no part of the interior was left dry. They'd consumed every drop of their sweet, hot tea and used every stitch of extra clothing in an attempt to ward off the cold. He'd never known such a long awful night as the hour hand of his wrist watch crawled towards morning.

But now that was all in the past, there was nothing like optimism, pleasure to assuage however awful recent memories were. He couldn't but admire, hand it to Chief Inspector Moran and Sergeant Young. What a team they were! Together it wasn't an exaggeration to say they were almost revered in the station. Young, experienced, grounded in common sense – a formidable presence in their midst. Moran, a thinker par-excellence, highly imaginative as tonight's events were proving, whose paternal attitude to the staff- uniformed, detectives, administrative alike – made for a contented purposeful work force with one of the best crime apprehension rates in the Northumbrian Division.

He moved to lean his sturdy, six-foot frame against the irregular sand stone blocks of the bothy's side wall, the oblong face pensive. The two of them were his models! They represented the practical, brilliantly supplementing the theory he tussled with three nights a week. A product of the exceptional comprehensive in Hexham, Gore had joined the force at eighteen Now six years on he wanted promotion to CID. He was taking the exams- forensics, the psychology of interviewing etc- the Blackstone's manuals his bibles. He was determined to build a good life for he and Julie and, of course, the kids they so passionately wanted.

And the 'dynamic duo' as they were affectionately and covertly called just kept on stretching him. He'd been the subject of what could only be termed a tutorial three days ago. With Reggie at his side, Sergeant Young facing them and the Chief, smiling slightly, behind his desk, they'd been made to think fully about the task in hand.

"Tell us about the do's and don'ts then, young Jim," the sergeant said, his brown eyes twinkling, "when you're holed up in that ruin." It was vintage Young- using his Christian name, which he seldom did, to unsettle and test.

"We never place ourselves at any of the openings, windows or door. A white face can be clocked on the darkest night. And when the suspect appears we've got to maintain absolute silence. We only use a phone to alert yourselves when he is completely out of earshot."

"Good lad, but there's more isn't there.!"

"Yes, you need to know the direction the car takes when Driggs returns with the drugs, and the road number." Gore said, flourishing the ordnance survey map he'd just been given.

Young chuckled, his ruddy face creasing about the mouth and eyes, "He's learning isn't he, Reggie." he exclaimed, looking at the craggy, somewhat stolid face of the grey-haired constable. "Surveillance, report....nothing else...no apprehension until later We want every man-jack of the filth with the stuff in their possession. Understood!"

"Yes, sergeant." they said almost simultaneously.

"And it's vital you stay warm." Moran came in mildly for the first time. "Mavis will have flasks of tea and sandwiches ready when you report back; and it doesn't matter about uniforms, wear as many clothes as you like."

"A car will pick you up before it gets dark." Young said finally

Now they just had to wait until Driggs, complete with drugs, returned from the vicinity of the disused chimney. It was an imposing construction, off to their right and about a hundred yards further up the hill. He could see why the criminal had made it central to his plans. His first sight of the tall stack, a solitary landmark in the isolation of the moors, had made him recall a chemistry lesson almost a decade ago. When the teacher, probably conscious of the mining tradition in the area, had touched on lead smelting; the man had explained how using coke the process was basically one of oxidising the galena mineral then reducing it to the metal; how the resultant lead fumes were so poisonous they had to be led away from the furnace by underground flues for as much as a mile before they could be safely discharged to the atmosphere. Then finally – and this had riveted him – how boys were sent into the flues to collect the small amounts of silver, produced as a by-product of the smelting, which had condensed on the walls

Gore smiled mirthlessly – Driggs returning with his 'silver' might think he was home and dry, but that was far from the case. He would know that the low-life, Kerr had ratted on him so he couldn't head for his farm. To do so, with the drugs, would mean almost certain arrest. Therefore he would have to get rid of the cocaine in a hurry, and that was just what Moran was banking on. The clever money was on Driggs establishing himself at one of the two hotels on the east side of the moors, only a few miles away. From either of these he could re-supply his pushers and end up with a suitcase full of cash. One of the hotels was very nice, had a good restaurant which was in keeping with the man's tastes- so was thought the likely destination. But the 'jock', master of contingency planning as ever, had chosen to alert both managers.

A slightly lop-sided Driggs, carrying a bulky bag, materialised from the darkness, and Gore had to restrain himself from jumping to punch the air It was five past eight, and a minute later the man was past and, gravity assisted, was trundling down to the car. The head lamps came on and the engine started just as another snatch of moonlight suddenly revealed the white gash of Brean's teeth as he thumbed his mobile into life.

Lauder, his stance open, chipped the golf ball. It described an arc rising to a height of about six feet, bounced and then collided with the base of the apple tree he had been aiming at. That was much better, he thought; if he remembered to keep his hands in front of the ball and his head still while executing the shot, then he was altogether more accurate. He retrieved the ball, conscious of the old thought that whenever one aspect of the game improved it was usually the signal for another to deteriorate. He left the lawn, shoved the seven iron into his golf bag propped up against the car and entered the house.

The sound of a hair-dryer from upstairs indicated there were still a few minutes left before Aileen was ready, so he sat down and picked up the morning paper. He'd only skimmed over it earlier, diverted by the arrival of a friend's letter in the post. But the main news was worth returning to. The lurid headline read, "Farmer, Huntsman, Degenerate," and dealt with the Driggs' recent arrest on the grounds of drug trafficking.

The bald details had emerged two days ago. But now, it seemed, on the basis of information received from an eye witness the newspaper had been able to flesh out the sensational story. The report told of how the person concerned, a guest at the hotel had watched through a half-closed door as the chief CID officer delivered the memorable words, "Good evening, Mr Driggs – are you aware that the custodial sentence for bulk supplying class 'A' substances is of the order of fourteen years?" And how Driggs started to rise from the bed, on which there was an open suitcase, then flopped back ashen-faced. There was then a description of events in the ensuing hour, of how the man and his fellow guests were asked to remain in their rooms while the police made a series of arrests as Driggs' unwitting associates, arriving in five minutes intervals, asked for him at the hotel reception.

As the sound of the hair-dryer continued unabated upstairs Lauder turned to the paper's editorial. It too dealt with the Driggs scandal, and the hyperbole was intense. The writer quantified the size of the haul – half a million pounds worth of cocaine and cannabis in terms of street value, maintained in a few years time the amount would seem commonplace as the unregulated skies proved the new Klondike for drug importation. Then, much in the same vein, bludgeoned the local Hunt by stating that now the drug connection had compounded their earlier crimes was it not high time for society, rather than allowing politicians to meddle with the current Act, to strengthen it and ban the existence of the entire movement altogether.

Lauder put the paper down and looked thoughtfully out of the window. The journalist was, of course, referring to the pending Bill seeking to re-establish hunting rights. However with the furore of recent weeks the Government was beginning to back-track. There was ministerial talk of there not being sufficient time in the parliamentary programme to fit in the proposed legislation; there were comments about commissioning a study to see if the abolition of the Ban would have any effects in improving the rural economy. In short, with the Driggs factor persisting and further public damnation in the offing, the Coalition were procrastinating, a sure sign that they were on the brink of one of their regulation 'U' turns.

In fact, with them prolonging the issue, the politicians needed to accelerate or there would be nothing left to legislate over. If the meet he'd seen last weekend was typical of the national scene then the movement was in terminal decline. Six poker-faced riders – the hounds outnumbering them by something like four to one – had clip-clopped through a neighbouring village to a storm of protest. The saboteurs and antis, emboldened by the knowledge that the depleted numbers and media sensitivity of the huntsman would mean none of the usual physical abuse, gave full vent to their feelings. A tirade of jeers and taunts were directed against the riders, the sheer volume causing the horses to whinny and fight the reins. Even the die-hards amongst their dwindling supporters took stock and wisely steered clear.

Lauder knew that much of the Hunt's calamitous straits were ascribed to him. A rumour of his brush with Driggs was now about with the latter, unsurprisingly, cast as a piece of filth. And if he needed any confirmation of his status it had come on his return to the golf club two days ago. It was embarrassing. First in the locker room and then on the way to the first tee, he was almost besieged by well-wishers. To the extent that Peter, one of the three friends accompanying him, wryly remarked how there'd been much less fuss over a Ryder Cup player he recently saw. Then afterwards in the nineteenth – his ribs having proved equal to the task – it was much the same. More hand shakes, warm smiles, enquiries after his health – a constant stream of people arriving at his table to express their support.

But Lauder knew there was very much a reverse side to all the goodwill. He had made some terrible enemies. What some of the huntsmen felt towards him when they first discovered his identity was as nothing compared to how they saw him now. He was their bête noir, the individual who was responsible for their world, their way of life, crashing around them.

Lauder blinked and shook his head. It wasn't easy to reconcile the fact that he was hated – to know there were several people locally who detested him. And even more disturbing, there was within that number a small few who, besides wishing him harm, were prepared to engineer it.

The lounge door opened, and Aileen came in. She smiled at him and then turned to the wall mirror for a final inspection; dressed in grey slacks with a crimson turtle-neck sweater, both of which accentuated her figure; she looked gorgeous.

Lauder stood up, his sombre thoughts forgotten. "Is madam ready to strike the ball into the distant, blue yonder?" he enquired, grinning at her.

*

It was surprisingly warm for the time of year on the side of the gorge. Running in a south-easterly direction, the steep little valley afforded protection from the north and also the prevailing westerlies. A small stream tumbled through heather and pale washes of bracken on its way to the Tyne.

But the temperature and the scene were lost on Clive Henshaw. He sat with his back against one of the few trees growing there, smoking and racked by his thoughts.

He'd been glad to get out of the house this morning. In fact when he thought of it he had hardly used the place in the last month. He couldn't abide the cold desolate air of it, the clutter everywhere, the piles of unwashed dishes thronging the kitchen surfaces. He'd never realised how dependent he was on Elaine until she was no longer there.

Henshaw scowled and drew a hand across the two-day old stubble on his chin. His wife, nine years his junior, had proven even more traitorous than his so-called friends. She seemed to relish his misfortunes – wanted to kick him when he was down. Her words had been short and brutal when he arrived home to find the suitcases at the door and the taxi due. He could still vividly remember her icy manner that afternoon, the ugly look spoiling her pretty face as she said she'd never really liked him, that he was no good in bed and now that he could no longer provide, the marriage for her was over. He was livid, had raised his hand to strike her, and but for the taxi arriving would have had the satisfaction.

He'd long known she was a bitch, simply not realised the extent of it. But he hadn't wanted anything altered – the nice meals, being able to relax in a warm comfortable house after a day's work, the attractive woman next to him at Hunt social functions... They had more or less compensated for her bad temper, the effort of keeping her under control. He'd never so much considered the ending of their marriage. But Lauder had put paid to that, and several other bloody things too. The bastard had dropped a bomb on his life!

The business was ruined, the two shops boarded up and their leases for sale. His customers hadn't just dwindled away, they'd disappeared. The day the news got out he'd been released on bail pending trial, it started. First the counter sales began to nose-dive. Then came the phone calls from the businesses he supplied; usually polite, unlike the attitudes of most of the public, but the message depressingly the same. Hotel, restaurant owners – people he'd known for years, met socially – put their minions on the line to tell him that following a review they were intending to get their meat elsewhere. And towards the end of the week, a few days after his release, the business was dead. The streets in both quarters of town where he traded just as busy as ever, but no-one coming through his doors. And that way it had remained. What few visitors did enter his premises were either reporters or people out to insult him; one woman actually spat in his face and, raging, had to be pulled out of the shop by her husband. He was left with no alternatives; and a fortnight after being taken into police custody he sold on his freezer stock to a rival butcher and gave his five staff a week's notice.

In some ways though, the bitterest pill was the reaction of his local Hunt. The whole responsibility for the deepening mess they found themselves in had been firmly placed on his shoulders. The fact that he acted with the tacit approval of some of the senior members was conveniently forgotten. It mattered not that he hadn't so much as touched Lauder; that the lunatic Kerr, running amok, was the cause of the crisis. A well-regulated row of backs was represented to him – it was as if he'd never existed.

The new Master, Dodds had set the tone. The shit, thirsting to settle old scores, had excluded him at every level. He was immediately denied information about the times and places of meets; his personal files were returned from the Hunt office; the kennel man, Golightly – hanging onto his job by his fingernails – was instructed not to speak to him; then finally his membership fee was refunded.

It was crushing – soul destroying. He felt as if his life's blood had been turned off. Hunting had been his passion since he was a teenager. He was never happier than when in the saddle, hard on the heels of the hounds with a fox in sight. And in return he'd given; worked tirelessly for the Hunt, devoted thousands of hours of his spare time to its welfare. But now that counted as nothing. He'd been thrown out without so much as a discussion.

For a time he thought that if the organisation could weather the storm there might be some softening of attitudes to him. But again Lauder had scotched that. First his woman then he would appear on television or be in a newspaper providing some new slant on the night of the raid. The issue wouldn't go away, and if it threatened to, there they would be again keeping the pot boiling. Davidson's treachery hadn't helped, of course, nor the latest amazing story of Driggs coming to grief. But assisted or not, Lauder had never relaxed his grip; each time he grabbed the headlines, driving himself and the Hunt further down into the mire. The bastard's skill in manipulating the media had been nothing short of uncanny. And he'd driven a wedge between Henshaw and his former pals, which he now knew would last as long as he drew breath.

Henshaw glanced at the '22' propped up against a slab of limestone protruding from the ground. Well, one thing was sure, he grimly thought, he would be drawing breath much longer than Mr 'bloody' Lauder. He couldn't remember when he actually decided on the 'accident'. It might have been when he watched the programme which reconstructed events that night; it might have been his mind finally acknowledging he would never take part in a Hunt again; or was it when he realised his present status could be described in four words: criminal – bankrupt – divorcee – pariah? Whatever... the timing of the idea didn't matter. What mattered was that he was going to get even with Lauder. The turd had wrecked his life, now he was going to wreck his. It would gain him no benefit, of course – he knew very well what he'd lost was irrecoverable. But, he mused, a wintry smile alighting on his fleshy face, he would feel enormously better.

The incredible thing was that as soon as he resolved to do it, the how had followed shortly afterwards. Henshaw gazed at the dirty, grey ribbon of tarmac winding its precipitous way down the hill on the far side of the gorge. He had crossed that road a couple of miles further on every week for years. It was part of his regular routine seeking hay for his beloved hunter, as much as calling at the paper shop each morning. And last week, bound for the Hardy farm again, he'd driven across the intersection, then involuntarily slammed on his brakes.

About the only memorable saying his old man ever uttered was: "Worry a problem and the answer doesn't come – leave it fallow and the piece of the jigsaw will drop into place." And that was exactly what happened. He hadn't even been thinking about Lauder. But sitting at that crossroads with a tractor chugging up behind him he'd seen the trap from which the bastard couldn't possibly escape.

Lauder was a golfer, and the road running at right angles was the direct route from the hamlet where he lived to the local club. Moreover, a road so tricky on the stretch past the gorge that an unwary driver had crashed to his death there last winter!

He'd put his theory to the test last Saturday. The tee-off times, prominently displayed on the notice board of the Golf Club's foyer, showed when Lauder and his three cronies were playing. Then it had been a case of waiting and watching, and sure enough, hidden behind the tree he was sitting beside, he'd seen the swine ascending the hill opposite him.

And now three days later- according to the club starting

sheet and much earlier than he dared hope – Lauder and his partner were due to play in about twenty minutes. Henshaw stood up, his eyes fixing on the top of the road.

*

"Fancy forgetting my golf shoes," Lauder remarked, shaking his head. They'd made a couple of miles out of the village before he remembered bringing them home for cleaning and re-waxing.

"It's worrying that senility is becoming so entrenched," Aileen said tartly.

Lauder smiled. "Anyway," he replied, "there's nothing spoiling. We can get a later time – the course is hardly used on a Tuesday afternoon."

*

"Where is he... where is he?" Henshaw fumed, looking blackly towards the top of the hill. Lauder should have been here nearly ten minutes ago. Unseeingly he lifted a bottle of ginger beer to his mouth, and finding it empty, cursed, then threw it savagely to shatter against a nearby rock.

Suddenly the square jowled face relaxed, the bulging eyes contracted. After all, he told himself, there was no point in losing his temper at this, the eleventh hour. He'd been yearning to be in such a position since the receivers had arrived at his premises, since Elaine flounced to the taxi, since the Hunt had kicked him out, since he'd read the trial date on the Court summons. So now when the moment was so near, why get uptight? Lauder would come, he was probably just delayed. And then the bastard would die! So these last minutes, Lauder's last minutes, weren't to be wished away – they were to be enjoyed to the full.

Henshaw crouched down, one knee on the ground, to look along the rifle with the matt black silencer at its extremity, and then nodded his approval. The waiting was almost over, the plot primed and he just didn't see how he could fail. The gun pointed the hundred yards across the gorge to the third bend near the top of the hill. It was the tightest and most wicked curve on the whole descent. There the land fell precipitously away down a rocky slope, so sheer only a few scraggy bushed grew on it, to the stream sixty yards below. It was the ideal place for an accident, Lauder wouldn't stand a chance. Even at the modest speed he would be travelling, a front wheel burst followed a fraction of a second later by another shot through the windscreen would be deadly. The swine, unable to see and out of control, would be hurtling through space before he knew what happened.

A Vauxhall crested the sky-line, and Henshaw was suddenly flattening himself behind the rock. On that under-used road, the distinctive royal blue colour plus the hammering of his heart meant his vigil was finally over.

*

Lauder changed into third to negotiate the first of a series of bends he could see stretching downwards in front of him. There'd been heavy rain the day before and he noticed a section of the hard shoulder had subsided, leaving some of the marking posts angling crazily towards the gorge. The road was in a poor state too, with earth and gravel washed from the other side now covering parts of its surface. In fact, the thought hit him, the conditions were ideal for a terrible accident!

Immediately the unease which he'd felt earlier reared up. Perhaps it was his last thought, perhaps with Aileen at his side the sunlit day was too perfect, but he was suddenly aware of an acute sense of foreboding. He shifted nervously in his seat to quickly glance around him.

Something was glinting over there on the far side of the gorge; reflections, several of them, all coming from the same small area. Glass in such an untrodden spot – broken glass – but a hill farmer or hikers wouldn't pollute in that manner! Alarm bells began blaring in his mind, and even as he applied more brake and, neglecting convention, steered to straddle the middle of the road, the bullets came.

First the on-side tyre burst with a terrific bang. And hardly had he overcome the frozen incredulity of the initial shock to begin fighting the car's sideways impetus, when the windscreen shattered with a loud retort. Unable to see, he desperately punched the opaqueness in front of him, with Aileen recoiling and gasping her horror.

The Vauxhall developed a will of its own. With tyres screaming and skidding, the car corkscrewed towards the edge of the gorge until abruptly responding to the bias of brakes it slewed into a spin. A post went thudding into space as one wheel left the ground altogether and the rear end yawed over the brink. Wild-eyed, his breathing as if suspended, Lauder reacted. He wrenched the gear lever into second and trod on the accelerator. The remaining functional tyres bit and, amidst a reek of burning rubber, hurtled them laterally across the road to end in a shuddering halt inches from solid rock wall.

A terrible rage engulfed Lauder's whole being. "Keep your head low, Aileen, and slide out of the door on your side," he said in a voice which amazed him with its self-control.

White-faced and sobbing she did so; and he followed her, only pausing to remove the gun from the glove compartment. He joined her crouching beside the rear wheel arch.

"Don't ask me not to – we can't go on like this!" he rasped as she looked at him and the old army revolver in dismay.

"Who in God's name wants to harm you now, Iain?" she cried, the tears beginning to trickle down her cheeks.

"It must be Henshaw," Lauder answered, his tone brittle with anger. "He's gone mad – his troubles have tipped him over."

Then, softening momentarily, he raised his uninjured

hand to stroke the wetness away from her face. "Look," he said gently, "stay here and don't move. I'll be back."

Whether her outstretched hand was to embrace or retain him he was never to know, for evading it he broke into a flat-out run. Down the road he tore, twisting and turning. A bullet spurted at his feet and whined into the bank at the far side. Then he saw what he was looking for, a slope not so steep as that at the corner. He threw himself over the edge, feet first. Digging his heels in and trying to avoid the worst of the rock projections, he skidded crazily on the seat of his pants towards the valley below. His feet slammed squarely into a large rock and then he was tumbling the last yards. Head over heels he fell, attempting to shield himself as best he could. He smacked down into the coarse sand at the side of the stream.

Another bullet thumped into the ground near him. And Lauder, both shaken and bruised, but still holding the revolver in his bloodied right grasp, launched his protesting body into a second twisting run. One, two, three – accelerate; one, two, three, four – decelerate then sprint in another direction. "The gunman always aims slightly in front of a moving target so keep altering the direction and speed of your advance. Once he becomes uncertain, you start winning," the NCO had hammered at them. And never was advice proving more apt, Lauder wildly thought as he suddenly slowed to hear a shot whine through the space just ahead of him. He lunged out of the shallow stream and sped across the valley floor, twisting and deliberately exaggerating his movements.

Henshaw was panting with distress. He wiped a hand across his sweating brow as he saw Lauder begin ascending his side of the hill. It was all going horribly wrong, he agonised. First he'd never bargained on him being accompanied; he hadn't seen his woman, partially hidden by the sun visor, until he loosed off the second shot. And now what the police would have dismissed as a tragic accident on a dangerous piece of road was turning into a nightmare. A nightmare where Lauder, clutching a gun, thirsting for his blood and seemingly unstoppable, was closing in on him. Rapidly losing what little remained of his nerve, he half raised himself to train the rifle on the darting advance figure.

Lauder felt a bullet pass perilously close to him as for the first time he glimpsed Henshaw silhouetted against the sky-line and firing from the shoulder. It flashed through his mind that unless he found cover he wouldn't survive another ten seconds, and desperately spurting about fifteen yards he hurled himself into the protection of a large boulder. He sagged down, his breath coming in laboured gasps.

It was Lauder's anger that dispelled his physical discomfort. If anything it was more intense now that he had a moment to consider. He could to a small extent understand Henshaw's twisted thinking. The man's life had disintegrated – a domino effect of calamity upon calamity for which he was thought responsible. But for Henshaw to involve Aileen was worse than despicable. Clearly the man was completely unbalanced and therefore had to be stopped. He yanked back the hammer on the revolver and edged to the side of the rock.

He knew exactly the sort of tactics he was going to employ, and spotting Henshaw's frame partially exposed, he fired. He was moving even before the whiplash crack died away, even before the gun stopped writhing in his hands. Running pell-mell, he covered about twenty yards to fling himself behind another rock. The softening-up process had started!

Henshaw cowered against the wall of his shelter. He'd never been fired at before, and he found the experience dreadful. The tiny fragments of stone now irritating his left eye showed how dangerously close Lauder's shot had been. He risked a feverish glance. There was nothing to be seen. Then suddenly a movement behind a boulder to the right of him not the one he'd looked at, and a second bullet ricocheted past him. Terrified, he threw himself flat.

Shaking uncontrollably, Henshaw got to his knees. His

flat cap was lying beside him; there was dirt in his hair, he could taste it, and his dark green coat was covered. "Christ," he gibbered, the bugger was doing as he pleased with him. Unless he did something, and quickly, he was finished.

It was that thought, self-preservation, which checked his panic and forced him to think objectively. In an instant of frightening clarity he saw that to survive there was only one option open to him. Lauder mustn't advance any further. He was hidden behind the start of a long, almost unbroken chain of limestone which stretched to the summit of the hill. So he must nail him where he was, otherwise Lauder would use the cover to get round the side of him, and then... Henshaw shivered visibly; he didn't care to think more.

Two shots – two misses, Lauder thought, then seeing a stone lying near him decided it was time to bring the whole appalling business to a head. It was an old trick but still a good one. Henshaw's position was about twenty yards above him, and if he could lure the rat sufficiently out of his hole, then he was fairly sure he could disable him. Steadying himself, he grasped the stone in his left hand.

Henshaw could hear his heart booming as the sweat coursed down his body and he watched. Silence – nothing – only the Vauxhall angled across the road, an oddity in an otherwise rural scene. Suddenly there was the clatter of stone upon stone, again not in the area he'd been watching, but further away to the right. It was just what he suspected would happen. Lauder using the chain of low-lying rock was creeping upwards in a bid to outflank him. Desperate to punish him, Henshaw half raised himself, his rifle aimed at a large fissure in the limestone table where Lauder must surely appear. The next moment there was a blur of movement out of the corner of his eye, and he was slammed backwards to the ground by a terrific blow to his right shoulder.

"Never leave your cover until you're certain the enemy

is down. Too many have paid admiring the supposed results of their handiwork." And automatically obeying another lesson from the past, Lauder ducked smartly down, He was confident he had hit Henshaw – he'd aimed to wing him and the man had dropped like a log. But he mustn't be hasty, the eye could be deceived. For all he knew Henshaw might have feigned collapse and was now poised waiting for him to make a wrong move. Deliberately suppressing the first stirrings of relief, he began to carefully crawl behind the line of rock leading upwards.

Henshaw's one conscious thought that transmitted his hell was to get away. To put as much distance between himself and this devil as he possibly could. He had to somehow make it to his his feet and then he might just stand a chance of escaping over the hill. The blood welling from beneath his collar bone, his breath coming in tortured gasps, he began to pull himself up using the elbow of his good arm as a pivot. He almost made it... But inches away from a sitting position, he wobbled, his weight suddenly transferred and he crashed down sideways on his injured shoulder. A new and even more refined agony speared through Henshaw's body; the sky above whirled, blackened and then fell enveloping him.

The figure of Lauder kicking his rifle away swam into view as he regained consciousness. The man then turned to lean over him, the pistol still clutched in his hand. Henshaw closed his eyes, knowing what must come next. He felt strangely calm – his life was next to nothing anyway, and there would be instant release from the God-awful pain.

Nothing – no click of a hammer retracting, no whirr of a chamber re-aligning; just a series of high pitched bleeps which he couldn't quite place. He weakly turned his head to see Lauder raise the mobile to his mouth, then begin speaking...

END

Lightning Source UK Ltd.
Milton Keynes UK
UKOW02f0518180616

276561UK00002B/3/P